"You pla[nned] didn't you?"

Devon tried to sit up, pulling her blouse around her. "This little seduction scene."

He wouldn't let her go. "I didn't walk in here expecting this, if that's what you mean. If you hadn't thrown yourself in my arms, I'd have said hello and gone upstairs to unpack. It's a bit late to play the innocent."

Her voice was tense. "I changed my mind, Jon."

"I see." His tone was dry as he stood up and rebuttoned his shirt. "It's your choice, Devon. I thought you'd made it, but apparently you still want to play games. When you change your mind about wanting to sleep with me—you'd better be convincing."

So much for your dreams, Devon, she told herself. *You thought you were different, that he really did care about you. What a fool you are!*

Come
Next Summer

Leigh Michaels

Harlequin Books

TORONTO • NEW YORK • LONDON
AMSTERDAM • PARIS • SYDNEY • HAMBURG
STOCKHOLM • ATHENS • TOKYO • MILAN

Original hardcover edition published in 1985
by Mills & Boon Limited

ISBN 0-373-02748-6

Harlequin Romance first edition February 1986

In memory of Edwin D. Lemberger
1906-1983
who shared with me the joy of politics

———————————◆———————————

Printed in U.S.A.

CHAPTER ONE

DEVON had planned to get up early that January morning. 'Not, however, quite this early,' she firmly told her Siamese cat. Cyan merely stared at her with innocent blue eyes, sat down on the pillow next to Devon's nose, wrapped her sable-brown tail elegantly round her cream-coloured body, and patiently washed her paws. Her statement was made; it was breakfast time.

Devon groaned, turned over on the couch and concentrated on going back to sleep. It was useless, though; Cyan had made up her mind.

Devon was reaching for her robe when a voice from the doorway said cautiously, 'Dev? Are you awake? I've got coffee for you.' The voice was followed by a small-boned, dark-haired girl in a quilted pink dressing-gown. She set a tray down on the coffee table and curled up in a chair across from Devon's makeshift bed. 'It's snowing,' she announced baldly.

'That's exactly what I didn't want to hear.'

Julie shrugged. 'It should make apartment hunting easier. No one else will be out.'

Devon reached for the coffee mug, already creamed and sugared to her taste. 'Everyone else already has an apartment,' she pointed out. 'With classes starting on Monday, everyone but me is already settled in. Why wasn't I smart enough to come back early?'

Julie shrugged. 'It wouldn't have made any difference. There isn't much turnover between autumn and spring semesters; you know that, Devon. Just people like you, who were gone in the autumn to do their practise teaching. A few here and there drop out, but almost everyone sits tight till spring.'

'Why do you always have to be so darn logical about everything, Julie?'

'It comes naturally,' Julie grinned. 'How did you like the party last night?'

Devon sank back against the pillows, pulling the blankets up around her. 'I met Mister Right at the punch bowl.'

Julie was undisturbed. 'You've done that at least three times a year since I've known you, Devon.'

'No, really! This time is it. I'm positive.' The cat yawned and then leapt up on her shoulders, curling around her neck like a fur collar and purring into her ear. 'Darn it, Cyan, I'll feed you when I'm ready,' Devon scolded. 'He's the ultimate Viking, Julie. Six-feet-one and curly blond hair and gorgeous big blue eyes . . .'

'And probably not a brain worth mentioning.'

'On the contrary! He's a graduate student—working for a masters in political science.'

Julie shrugged. 'Oh, well! Political science!'

'Just because you think biology is the only science there is . . .' But Devon was smiling. Julie had teased her about her boyfriends since the day they had moved into their first cramped dormitory room together.

Cyan licked her ear, and Devon jumped up. 'All right, cat. Breakfast it is. And then off to hunt an apartment for us.'

Julie looked gloomy. 'I wish I could invite you to stay here,' she said. 'But . . .'

'Julie, I'm grateful to your parents as it is. Loaning me their study for a few days is more than generous, considering the cat and all my junk.' She waved a hand to the boxes piled against the opposite wall. 'And I'd have to get my own place after the wedding, anyway. I can't stay with your parents after you're married.'

Julie sighed. 'You could move in with David and me.'

'Exactly what the newlyweds need.' Her smile was fond. 'Just because you're marrying my brother doesn't mean you have to take care of me, you know.'

'I worry about you.'

'I know, Julie. But I moved out of Aunt Eleanor's house the minute I was old enough. I've been on my own for years now.'

'Speaking of your Aunt Eleanor—her guest list for the wedding is getting longer by the day.'

'Ignore her,' Devon recommended. 'I don't know how you are going to stand living with her, Julie.'

'It's free, and that helps a lot,' Julie pointed out.

'David was always her favourite,' Devon reflected. 'I never could get away with the things he could.'

'David can do no wrong,' Julie agreed. 'Sometimes she thinks I'm all right because David couldn't possibly make a mistake. But most of the time she just thinks I'm not good enough for him.'

'Well, I adore my big brother just as much as Aunt Eleanor does, but I know that you're far too good for him.'

Julie giggled, spoiling the effect. 'He just knows how much I'm costing him right now. The wedding coming up, and med school in the autumn . . .'

'He's no dummy. If he supports you for the next five years, he can retire in comfort on a doctor's income. His own private doctor. Amazing that Aunt Eleanor doesn't see that.'

'Oh, she doesn't approve of girls who think they want to be doctors. She'd rather I stay home and have babies—after the wedding, of course. I plan to spend most of my time on campus.'

'And the professors all think you're such a star student. Someday I'll tell them why you're really devoting all that time to your labwork,' Devon threatened. 'Besides, if I lived here I'd have to have a car. It must be five miles over to the campus, and I can't hike that in this weather. Did you say it was snowing?'

'Not quite a blizzard, but close enough.' Julie's voice was cheerful. 'We could go build a snowman right now.'

'Hardly my idea of fun. Why didn't I go to college in Arizona?'

'Because this one gives you free tuition. Remember?'

'How could I forget? At any rate, I have to find an apartment close to campus, and I will either have to pay a premium price, or settle for a dump.'

'Probably both,' Julie said cheerfully.

Devon was rummaging through the pile of boxes, looking for Cyan's cat food. Even in a terrycloth bathrobe she succeeded in being casually elegant. 'As long as it doesn't have cockroaches,' she announced.

'Darling, every apartment within two miles of campus has cockroaches. It's a legal requirement.'

'Must you sound so darn pleased about it?'

'If you can't find anything, we'll work it out here. It would be fun to have you around all the time—we could stay up all night and gossip.'

'It might work till the wedding,' Devon said. 'But after that you'd be tripping over me every time you turned around.'

'It would be fun, though—just like the old days in the dormitory. Do you remember the weekend nobody called and we demanded that the telephone company send a repairman out so we could be sure the darn 'phone worked?'

'And when he told us it was not out of order, we were so depressed that we left fake messages to cheer ourselves up?' Devon searched for her favourite jeans, washed so many times that they were soft and faded.

'That was before the fraternity houses found you, and I became your social secretary.' Julie looked a little disappointed.

Devon flipped her golden-blonde hair back over her shoulder and started to brush it, long strokes that left it gleaming and silky as it streamed halfway down her back. 'If I'm the one who got popular,' she pointed out gently, 'why is it that you're going to be the bride, and I'm the maid of honour?' She pointed across the tiny room to the long white gown on the dressmaker's dummy, bristling with pins.

'That's easy. You have a basic distrust of men.'

Devon's brush stopped in the middle of a stroke. 'That's ridiculous, Julie. I've dated a hundred guys.'

Julie nodded. 'And just as soon as one of them starts to get serious, you tell him very sweetly that you'd like to be his friend. It comes from your fear of rejection, actually. Your father deserted you when you were a child, therefore you think no man can be trusted.'

Devon slowly started brushing her hair again. 'And when did you decide to become a shrink?' she asked sweetly.

Julie shrugged. 'That insight didn't take a shrink, hon. That's beginning psychology. You heard the same lectures I did, but you weren't listening.'

'Well, diagnosing my hang-ups isn't getting me an apartment.' She put the brush down.

'Aunt Eleanor has one more bedroom.'

'Living with her is out of the question.'

'But she's your aunt,' Julie objected.

'She was so delighted when I moved out that she would see me living in a garbage can before she'd extend her hospitality for more than a couple of days. She doesn't approve of my cat. To say nothing of all the men in my life—she's scared that I'm some kind of loose woman.' The last sentence was muffled as Devon pulled a turtleneck sweater over her head. 'And I'm not about to give up my social life to please her.'

'Well, at least she does approve of your career choice. English teachers are a lot higher in her estimation than girls who want to be doctors.' Julie imitated Aunt Eleanor's tone. 'She thinks I'm only going to school for fun.'

'As if it was that easy to get in,' Devon mused.

'If we could afford it, we'd move in a minute. But we're stuck with Aunt Eleanor till I graduate. Right now it looks like forever.'

'Maybe someone will die and leave you and David a

million dollars.' Devon draped a chunky gold necklace over the turtleneck and reached for the matching earrings.

'No one I know has a million dollars,' Julie mused. 'It never fails to amaze me; you can get dressed in five minutes and you always look like the front cover of *Vogue*. I'm going over to the lab in a couple of hours.'

'It's Christmas break!'

Julie shrugged. 'Somebody has to feed the rats. Do you want a ride?'

Devon shook her head. 'I'll catch a bus. I got some addresses from the student housing office yesterday, and I want to check them out first thing. And since it's Friday, I have to locate something today so I can move this weekend.'

'Do you want to go to a movie tonight? Maybe David will take us.'

'Oh—I can't, Julie.'

'The Viking?' Julie deduced shrewdly.

'His name is Matt and he's taking me to the city symphony over at the performing arts hall.'

'I know. Even Vikings have occasional flashes of good taste. Just be careful, Dev. You don't know much about him.'

'How much trouble can I get into at a concert? I can look out for myself.'

Julie looked dubious. 'Good luck on the apartment hunting.'

Julie had good reason to sound doubtful about her chances, Devon decided when by late afternoon she had exhausted her list. It seemed that there was not a single apartment for rent within walking distance of the campus. Devon scratched off the last address, sighed, and dropped the list into a garbage can.

It was starting to get dark, with the street lights flickering to life and reflecting off the swirling snowflakes. The day was gone, and she was out of luck. She shrugged snow off the shoulders of her long wool coat and went into The Portable Pie Company to take a break.

Portable Pies specialised in pizzas-to-go, but as the primary gathering spot for the university crowd, it carried a menu as diverse as the student body. Devon sat down at a small table by the front window and when the smiling waitress came by, she ordered a mug of hot apple cider.

The snow was piling up, drifting from a heavy grey sky in huge clumps of flakes. Another hour of this, Devon thought, and traffic would grind to a halt. Already there was no evidence of old, dirty snow left under the fresh blanket of white.

She stirred her hot cider with a cinnamon stick. A perfect day to be inside, she thought, and watching the snow from a warm kitchen heavy with the smell of baking bread. Not a perfect day to be without a kitchen or even a loaf of bread to call her own.

Just what would she do if she couldn't find a place to live? Imposing on Julie's parents any longer was unthinkable. Besides, Devon thought, she wanted a place of her own.

She stared into her cup and wondered if there was a dormitory room still available. She hadn't lived in a dorm since her freshman year; that was where she had met Julie. The dorms were expensive, and the food was awful. But it might be her only choice.

'You look very thoughtful.'

Devon glanced up over the rim of her mug at a tall, dark-haired man, pipe in one hand, a wrapped taco in the other, who stood beside her table.

'May I sit down?' he asked, and did. 'It's crowded today.'

Devon looked around. It was, indeed, crowded— unusually so for late afternoon. Students were sheltering from the snow and catching up on the news from Christmas break. She shrugged and made no comment. Anyone with manners would eat his taco in silence, she thought.

He didn't. 'Are you a student here?'

She stirred her cider and didn't look at him. 'Yes.' The syllable was clipped and unfriendly. Too many men had tried to pick Devon up for her to fall for that sort of approach.

He fell silent, and she congratulated herself.

Then he said, 'Fascinating snowstorm.'

Devon pulled her attention away from the window. She'd been idly looking at the big white house across the street. 'Fascinating? How could a snowstorm be fascinating?'

'It must be. You're paying a great deal of attention to it.'

She looked him over carefully, employing a technique learned years ago. Devon's long cool stare was guaranteed to reduce the brashest of fraternity men to quivering jelly in a matter of thirty seconds.

It did nothing to this man. She stared at him long enough to decide that his face was ruggedly interesting rather than handsome, that his nose looked as if it had been broken at least once, that he had the broad shoulders of a football player, and that his dark brown hair was carefully cut and inclined to curl. He was older than the usual campus man—probably a graduate student, she decided.

He merely ate the taco without a trace of self-consciousness, crumpled the paper, and picked up his pipe. When Devon, still without a word, turned her attention back to the window, he said, 'May I conclude that you liked what you saw?'

She started to ask him if he was as conceited as he sounded, but her attention was drawn back to the house across the street. The big, lighted window that she had been looking at longingly now displayed a sign that said, Apartment for Rent.

Devon ran for the door. The sign hadn't been there two minutes ago; that sort of luck came only once in a lifetime, and she was not going to hang about wondering what she should do.

She dodged cars across four lanes of traffic, ignoring a shout from the doorway of Portable Pies, and pulled up on the front porch of the big old house, out of breath. She pressed the doorbell and then leaned against the jamb. This had to be it; she had to be lucky this time. And what luck! The house had been one of the original mansions that lined the streets when the town was new; most of them had been torn down to make room for the campus. Even if the house had deteriorated, it would not be one of the small, boxy apartments that surrounded the university.

A voice came out of the dusk beside her. 'You'd better start being a little more careful.'

She looked up, startled. The dark-haired man was climbing the steps to the front porch. He came to stand beside her and pulled his pipe out of his pocket.

'In the dark, and with it snowing like this, drivers have more to do than watch out for careless pedestrians. By the way, I seem to owe you an apology.'

'You certainly do,' Devon snapped, all patience gone. 'And if you don't stop following me you'll be in for a lot more than an apology.'

He lifted an eyebrow and struck a match, trying to light the pipe. A gust of wind quenched the flame, and he sighed and dropped the matchbook back into his pocket. 'It isn't often that I have that effect on a woman, you see,' he added apologetically. 'Making her run out of a restaurant without paying for her apple cider.'

Devon's mouth dropped open, and she took a step towards the street. 'I didn't pay for it, did I?' she murmured.

'No, you didn't.'

She looked uncertainly from the house to the pizza parlour. If she went back to pay the bill, she might lose the apartment. But if she didn't . . .

'I took it as a compliment, actually.'

'You insufferably conceited...' Words failed Devon.

His dark eyes were sparkling. 'You really should be nice to me. I bought your cider.'

'Thank you.' It was grudging, and Devon fumbled in her pocket. 'I'll pay you back, of course.'

He waved it away. 'Apartment for rent, hmmm?' he said, reading the sign. 'Running into you might have been a stroke of luck after all. I've been looking for one.'

'Well, keep looking. This one is mine,' Devon announced.

'Not yet it isn't,' the dark-haired man said pleasantly.

The door opened a crack and before Devon could say a word, the man announced, 'We've come about the apartment.'

The elderly man at the door smiled. 'That was quick,' he said. 'The ad's just come out in tonight's paper. Would you come in, Mister...'

'Hardesty, Jon Hardesty.'

The landlord looked expectantly at Devon. 'Missus Hardesty?'

'Devon Quinn,' she said, thinking that if the apartment was advertised in the newspaper, there would be dozens of people wanting it. She'd have to move quickly.

'Dreadful weather, isn't it?' the landlord said. 'Just come this way. There's a separate entrance, of course, but I hate to go out in the cold, so I'll take you through. It's a very nice apartment, two bedrooms and bath upstairs and living room and kitchen downstairs.'

'That's an unusual arrangement,' Jon Hardesty said. He was studying the long hallway, with its high ceiling and elaborately carved woodwork.

'Yes, I don't know why they split the house vertically like that, but it makes a pretty apartment. The previous owners did the remodelling. I believe her mother moved in with them.'

'That explains everything,' Jon smiled. Devon could have hit him; he and the landlord seemed to be on the same wavelength.

It was a pretty apartment. The bedrooms were large and airy; the bathroom old-fashioned but recently redecorated, and the kitchen seemed to have been designed for her. It wasn't all furnished, but there was enough furniture to get by with. But it was awfully large, and the rent would probably be high. Then she scolded herself. No matter what it cost, she would grab it. She wasn't in a position to be choosy, Devon thought as she poked about the kitchen cabinets.

Then, abruptly, she realised that she couldn't hear the landlord and the man who had called himself Jon Hardesty. She slammed the cabinet door and rushed into the living room. If he managed to rent the apartment out from under her, she'd have no one but herself to blame.

'I'll leave you to look it over,' the landlord was saying. 'I'll be across the hall. I think I hear my telephone ringing.'

As soon as the door closed behind him, Devon said, 'I'm going to rent this apartment, Mister . . . whatever your name is.'

'Hardesty. And you're welcome to try, Miss Quinn, because I also plan to rent it.'

She tried to reason with him. 'I've been looking all day, and I must have an apartment before Monday, when classes start.'

'Well, I've been looking all week, and I also must have a place to live before Monday. You said you're a student?'

'Yes. What possible difference could that make?'

'Then you must have all kinds of friends around campus. I, on the other hand, am brand-new in town and know no one. You probably have dozens of places to stay, but I have nothing.'

'Where have you been staying?' Devon asked irritably. 'If you've been here all week . . .'

'In a hotel. I'll only be here one semester, but the cost of a hotel room does add up over the course of a few months. That's why I should have the apartment.'

'Whatever happened to gentlemen?'

'That went out when equal rights came in.' He searched his pockets, found his pipe, put it between his teeth.

'I suppose you think that thing makes you look violently attractive,' she snapped.

He looked up over the bowl of the pipe with a smile. 'No. Just serious and thoughtful. He's asking four hundred a month, by the way.'

'Four hun . . .' Devon swallowed hard. It would be murderous to her budget; she had hoped to get by this semester without holding down a job. 'That's a little higher than I wanted to go, but I'll manage.' She stared at him fiercely.

'It is a bit steep,' he agreed. 'Of course, for this much space . . . Why do you need all the space, by the way? Got a boyfriend moving in with you?'

'Of course not.'

'I stand corrected. If you did, you wouldn't need two bedrooms.'

The landlord tapped on the half-open door. 'I don't mean to sound pushy,' he said, 'but there's a woman on the 'phone who wants to look at the place. I don't want her to come clear across town in this weather if it's going to be rented when she gets here. What shall I tell her?'

'We'll take it,' Jon Hardesty said. He didn't even turn around. The landlord smiled and backed out of the room.

Devon gasped. 'What do you mean, *we'll* take it?'

'Look—what was that unusual name of yours? Devlin?'

'Devon,' she snapped.

'We can stand here till midnight and argue about who's going to get this apartment, and in the meantime he'll rent it to someone else. At least we have now assured that we have an apartment to argue about.' He sat down and lit his pipe. When it was finally drawing to his satisfaction, he looked up. 'You may as well sit down,' he suggested mildly.

She ignored the suggestion. 'What do you propose we do about this—impasse?'

'I see nothing to propose. I have every intention of moving in here tomorrow.'

Devon put her hands on her hips. 'Well, so do I.'

He smoked quietly for a few minutes. 'And nothing will change your mind?'

'Nothing.'

'Then I think we should go sign the lease.'

'Just what does that mean?'

'A lease? It's a guarantee that . . .'

'I know what a lease is,' Devon said between gritted teeth.

He shrugged. 'Then there's just one question left. Do you want the front bedroom or the back?'

'You mean—both of us live here?'

'Why on earth not? There's plenty of room, and we could both benefit from splitting the rent.'

'Aunt Eleanor will never believe this.'

'You think that's going to be difficult. I have to explain it to my wife and three kids.'

'What?' Devon nearly shouted the word.

He nodded sadly. 'You know how it is. Can't move kids in the middle of a school year, and when I found myself suddenly without a job, I had to come where there was one.'

'You must be crazy to suggest something like this!'

He frowned. 'You're probably right. Can you supply me with character references? So I can show them to my wife, you understand.'

I've lost my marbles. That's the only explanation, Devon told herself as she sat through the first half of a concert that ordinarily would have absorbed her.

I signed my name to a six-month lease on an
apartment, and I'm sharing it with a man I never met
before today.

It sounded even worse when she stated it baldly like
that. He could be anything from an escaped rapist to
an undiscovered axe murderer, and she was moving in
with him in the morning.

She dragged her attention back to the orchestra hall.
The snow had tied up the city; attendance was sparse
and the crowd was scattered over the auditorium.

'They're good, aren't they?' Matt whispered,
bending his head towards her.

Devon nodded and tried to pay more attention. The
programme included Rachmaninov tonight, and the
stormy music should fit her mood perfectly, but she
found her attention wandering again just moments
later. Unable to concentrate on the music, she started
to study the crowd.

A bit later, Matt said, 'Look up in the box seats to
your left, Devon.'

Obediently, she did. 'Which one, Matt? I don't
see . . .'

'In the third box from the front. The silver-haired
man is Bob Dickinson. He's been in the United States
Senate so long that there isn't even a contest any more
when he comes up for a vote. I'd sure like to work for
him.' There was a tone of reverence in his voice.

But Devon wasn't listening. She was staring at the
other male occupant of the box.

'That's Jon Hardesty with him,' Matt went on. 'I
can't wait to meet him, either.'

The matron sitting in front of them turned to fix
Matt with a devastating glare, and he subsided.

So this Jon Hardesty is moderately famous, Devon
thought; and it seemed that neither rape nor axe
murder was his speciality, if he was hobnobbing with a
Senator. She glanced up at the box again. He certainly
looked important tonight; a well-cut tuxedo did
nothing to hide those broad shoulders, and though

Devon knew he wasn't truly handsome he was certainly attractive. The woman at his side added to the impression, as well; she was the most beautiful woman Devon had ever seen. Her black hair was coiled high on her head and her red dress sparkled under the lights. That, Devon thought, must be his wife—and no wonder she insisted on character references.

When intermission came Matt almost leaped out of his seat. 'I want to scrape an acquaintance with those two,' he announced. 'Are you coming?'

Devon didn't want to come face to face with Jon Hardesty in the lobby, but she also didn't want to explain her reluctance to Matt. So she shrugged and stood up. Besides, she might be able to get some information from him. 'Why is that name familiar? Hardesty, I mean.'

Matt was delighted to have an audience that he could instruct. 'Hardesty was a one-term U.S. Representative,' he said. 'He's from the southern part of the state, though; not your district at all. You do read the newspapers now and then?'

'Just because I'm studying English literature doesn't mean I read only Chaucer, Matt.'

He grinned. 'It's hard to believe you could live in this state and not know the name. He was defeated in the last election, because the presidential landslide hurt his party badly. He just left office the first of January. He'll be back, though.'

'So what is he doing here at the university?'

'He's one of the few Congressmen who is not an attorney—he started out as a professor of political science. So while he's waiting for his star to rise again, he's going to teach here. I've signed up for some of his graduate seminars.'

'You sound certain that he'll be back into politics.'

Matt grinned. 'You have heard of the Kennedy family?' he teased.

'I seem to vaguely recall them,' Devon said tartly. 'Is he related?'

'Only in spirit. Jon Hardesty's father is just about as determined as Joe Kennedy was to put a son in the White House.'

'Missus Hardesty would make a lovely First Lady.'

'What? Oh, you mean the woman he's with.'

'That was the one I was thinking of,' Devon murmured.

'She's not his wife.' Matt stepped into a gap in the crowd around the two objects of his attention, pulling Devon along with him.

Devon didn't resist. So the lovely lady wasn't his wife. She wondered what his wife was like, and whether she minded being left behind. She had to be young, certainly. He wasn't much more than thirty himself. And to have three school-age children. They must have been high school sweethearts.

She and Matt were now just a couple of rows back in the crowd, near enough for Devon to hear clearly as the dark-haired woman said peevishly, 'Let's go back and sit down, Jon.'

'In a minute, Margo.' He was still shaking hands, and Matt inched his way through the crowd.

'Dr Hardesty!' he said. 'I'm Matt Lyon, and I'll be in your graduate seminars this semester. What do you think about . . .'

Devon lost track of the question about halfway through, but Jon Hardesty was patience itself. It's as though there was no one else around, she thought, surprised at the degree of attention he was giving Matt. But of course that was a politician's chief asset, being able to make each person feel valuable.

'Jon!' The dark-haired woman tugged at his arm. Devon thought he looked a little disappointed as he turned to her. 'Margo . . .' Then he saw Devon, and his eyes started to sparkle dangerously.

'Dr Hardesty,' she said coolly, offering her hand.

To her utter astonishment, he raised it to his lips with a flourish. 'Miss Quinn,' he murmured as he kissed the back of her hand. He turned it over and started to press his lips to the sensitive palm.

She snatched it out of his grip.

'Jon!' the dark-haired woman said again. This time she sounded angry.

'I'm coming, Margo. Excuse me, Matt. Miss Quinn, I'll see you tomorrow.' They moved off through the crowd.

'Well!' Matt stared down at Devon. 'Aren't you a dark horse? I thought you didn't know anything about Jon Hardesty.'

'I don't, Matt. I just happened to meet him today, that's all.'

Matt didn't pursue it. 'Little Margo is a lousy campaigner, isn't she?' he commented as they returned to their seats. 'A woman who can't shake a hundred hands in a theatre lobby won't be much use to him on the campaign trail.'

'I'm sure she has other attractions for Dr Hardesty.'

Matt looked at her curiously. 'Not the least of which is that she's Bob Dickinson's daughter. Funny that she isn't a hand-shaker.'

'Perhaps she feels there's no point to it, now that he is out of office.'

'How innocent can you be?' Matt asked. 'Once a politician, always a politican.'

The conductor came on stage, and Matt let the subject drop as the second half of the concert began. But Devon thought about it the rest of the evening. And every time she looked up at the box seats, she saw Jon Hardesty's profile.

And she nibbled on a manicured fingernail and wondered what would happen to her when she moved into that apartment.

CHAPTER TWO

As the battered station wagon pulled up behind Devon's new apartment, the young man who was driving let out a long, low whistle.

The other man, in the passenger seat, breathed, 'Look at that gorgeous car.'

Devon wriggled on her precarious perch among boxes piled in the back of the wagon and looked. It was a brand-new, low-slung sports car, jade green with a sun roof and probably every accessory Detroit could think of. And it must mean that Jon Hardesty was already in residence.

Damn, she thought. It was only ten in the morning. She had been certain she could get moved in first. Now she would have to introduce Brad and Roger to Jon Hardesty.

She wished that her brother David had come along; it would have made it easier since he already knew what little she did about her new roommate. David and Julie had argued and pleaded and demanded for hours last night. Finally they had given up when Devon pointed out that she had signed a lease and was committed to paying rent on the apartment whether she lived there or not. Julie had thrown up her hands in despair and said, 'You can always come back here when it falls apart, Dev.' David had reserved judgment, but there had been concern in his eyes.

David would have been prepared to meet Jon Hardesty this morning. But he'd had to work, and Roger and Brad didn't know anything about her new living arrangements.

'Roger,' she said quietly. 'And Brad . . . Perhaps I should warn you . . .'

'What?' Roger asked as he backed the station wagon

to within inches of the door. 'Are you dating the guy who drives the luscious car? That's no news at all.'

'Not exactly. I'm going to be living with the guy who drives it.'

The car came to a sudden, shrieking halt. Roger stared at her in the driving mirror. Brad twisted around in the seat. 'You're what?' they said, almost in unison.

'That's not quite right either,' Devon amended. 'I'm sharing an apartment with him, that's all.'

Roger looked at Brad and said, 'The same Devon who never let me get past a good night kiss?'

Brad said, 'Don't look at me. I, too, was invited to be her friend.'

'And that's what you are, guys. You're good friends. I wouldn't ask you to help me move if you weren't.' But the near-echo of what Julie had said just yesterday rang disturbingly in her ears. Did she wear a kind of hands-off message, warning men not to get too close?

'Thank you, Devon.' Brad bowed from the waist, the best he could do in the small car. 'So, since we're friends, let's go inspect this guy and see where we went wrong.'

'You didn't go wrong!' Devon wailed. 'I'm not living with him . . .'

'You just said you were,' Roger pointed out.

'We're splitting the rent so we can afford to live here. It's a different thing altogether. Can you get it through your thick head?'

'I'll try,' Roger promised. He got out of the car. 'What goes in first?'

'The plants,' Devon decided. 'The Boston fern goes in the corner of the living room and the creeping Charlie above the kitchen sink.'

'I can never tell them apart.'

'This is the Boston fern,' Devon said tartly, putting it in his hand. 'And here is Charlie. Left hand to the kitchen, right hand to the living room. Got it?'

'Got it,' Roger agreed. 'Nice apartment, Devon,' he said as they entered the kitchen.

'Devon always manages to land on her feet,' Brad agreed as he came in with a big box. 'Where does this go?'

'What does it say on top?' Devon asked. She took it out of his hands and set it on the kitchen table.

Brad steadied the chair that Roger had climbed on to hang the creeping Charlie above the sink. 'Do you want all the other plants in the living room?'

'How many are there?' asked a polite voice from halfway down the stairs.

Devon had tried to prepare herself, but she still jumped at the sound of his voice. She turned slowly around.

'Good morning, Devon,' Jon said as he came on down the stairs. 'Good morning, gentlemen.'

Some sort of introduction seemed in order. 'Brad, Roger, Jon Hardesty.'

'We're Devon's ex-boyfriends,' Roger volunteered. 'If you don't treat her right, we'll haunt you.' Devon could have thrown something at him.

'Have you formed a club?' Jon opened a cabinet door and reached for a coffee mug.

'I'm going to go carry in my things,' Devon announced. 'If you three want to stand here and chat, go right ahead.'

Three trips later Brad and Roger were still hanging plants by the sunny bay window. 'I didn't know I was going to be living in a tropical rain forest,' Jon commented from the couch, where he was stretched out comfortably.

'Nobody asked you to.' Devon set Cyan's cat carrier down in the centre of the room and opened it. 'We're all moved again,' she crooned to the frightened Siamese. 'Nobody's going to make you go anywhere for six months, baby.'

Jon raised up on an elbow. 'Make that a tropical rain jungle,' he said. 'I don't seem to remember anyone talking about a cat. What happens, my dear Devon, if I am allergic to cats?'

Cyan let out a piteous meow and climbed into Devon's arms. 'Then, my dear Jon, you will probably sneeze a lot in the next six months. I met Cyan before I met you, and frankly, if one of you has to go . . .'

'I get the picture. Fortunately, I am not allergic to cats.'

Devon set Cyan on her shoulder and went to the kitchen to unpack boxes. The cat jumped down and huddled under a chair, surveying her new home with wide, unblinking blue eyes.

'What did you say its name is?'

'Cyan. It's the colour of her eyes.'

'They look blue to me.' He sat down at the small table. 'Just don't put the cat food where I might mix it up with my breakfast cereal. I'm not terribly alert first thing in the morning.'

She opened all the cabinet doors. 'I'll take this set of shelves, and you can have the ones on the other side of the range, and then neither of us will have to worry.' She opened the refrigerator. 'And we'll split the refrigerator right down the middle.'

'I already stocked up on staples this morning. Help yourself.'

'So did I,' Devon snapped. 'And I'd just as soon keep things separate. You bought margarine, for heaven's sake.'

'Yes. Am I going to be hung at dawn for it?'

'I do not use margarine, or coffee whitener, or any of those other chemical substitutes that threaten to put the American cow out of business.'

'Butter is expensive.'

Devon slammed the refrigerator door. 'So are sports cars, but I notice you don't drive the economy version.'

'Two points for you,' Jon said appreciatively.

Brad and Roger rattled down the stairs. 'That's everything, Dev,' Brad said. 'Your bedroom is full of boxes, though, I draw the line at unpacking for you.'

'Thanks, guys.' She crossed the kitchen and put an arm around each of them. 'I appreciate all the help.'

'It's nice to know we're still good for something, even if you are living with another man,' Roger mused.

Devon glanced over at Jon, who leaned back in his chair, a wicked gleam in his dark eyes.

'Want to go to the basketball game tonight?' Roger asked.

'Sure,' Devon said. 'It will be a treat to see a good game.' She walked out to the car with them.

'I'll pick you up about seven,' Roger announced, and dropped a casual kiss on her cheek.

'Despite it all, I kind of like him, Devon. Your Jon, I mean.' Brad kissed her other cheek and got in the car. 'He didn't get upset when Roger threatened him, and that's a good sign.'

'He's not mine,' Devon pointed out. 'And if I could get rid of him, I would. See you tonight.'

After they drove off, she took a deep breath of the frosty air, wishing she didn't have to go back in. But her sweatshirt was not heavy enough to hold out the winter cold, and her breath hung like a cloud in the air.

Jon was sitting at the kitchen table with a fresh cup of coffee and a glazed doughnut.

'I have never seen one woman with so much stuff,' he announced. 'How did you get it all in one carload?'

'Brad and Roger have moved so many times they're expert packers.'

'How handy for you. I was a little surprised that you didn't bring along the young man from last night. What was his name?'

'I'm fairly sure you remember his name. It's Matt Lyon.'

'Or weren't you prepared to introduce him to the old boyfriends?' Jon guessed shrewdly. 'Do they have regular meetings, and elect officers and all? I can't imagine there are only two of them.'

'All of them are just friends now.'

'And Brad and Roger are the squad in charge of moving you around.'

'They're roommates. I introduced them.'

'Of course. How lucky for me that I was already here. Otherwise you'd have had my room filled with . . . whatever all those boxes have in them.' He waved a hand towards his half of the countertop. 'Have a doughnut. If you eat them, that is. Are glazed doughnuts chemically impure?'

Devon smiled reluctantly. 'Doughnuts are all right now and then. Though I must admit I usually make my own.'

'You make doughnuts? Good, you owe me one. Perhaps I should have asked—are you a vegetarian too?'

'No. I like a rare steak. And that's what they've been lately, too. Rare.' Devon selected a doughnut and hunted for her coffee mug in the box on the counter. Three boxes later she still hadn't found it.

Jon quietly got up and handed her one from his side of the cupboard. 'You can use my television anytime you want too. Except when the Super Bowl is on.'

She stared at the cup and then smiled reluctantly. 'Thanks. I guess I was a little obnoxious.'

'Quite a little,' he agreed. He sipped his coffee and looked at her innocently over the rim.

'Help yourself to my stereo,' she said, feeling a little foolish.

'Thank you,' he said gravely. 'I'll treat it with utmost caution. You aren't used to sharing an apartment, are you?'

'Not for a long time.'

'I will attempt to keep that in mind. You've been away from the university for a while?'

'I did my practise teaching last semester, and I had to move halfway across the state to find a high school that had room for a novice teacher.'

'English literature?'

'Yes. How did you know that?'

Jon shrugged. 'It was obvious from the boxes of books on the living room floor. A lot of students have to read Chaucer and Milton—but not many of them keep the books when the course is over. And the leather-bound Rupert Brooke gave it away.'

'I guess you're right. Very few of my students felt as I do about the classics.'

'It's a problem all teachers face. No one is as excited about our subjects as we are.'

'And then there is the lack of jobs.'

'Are you trying to find one?'

'I graduate in May, and I'm only beginning to realise that English lit was a poor choice. Plus I didn't take college very seriously for the first couple of years, so there are a lot of people out there whose qualifications look better than mine.' She refilled her coffee cup.

'What about you? Are you happy to be back to teaching?'

He reached for another doughnut. 'You've apparently picked up a little information since yesterday.'

'It wasn't hard to get. Matt was quite willing to fill me in. He's excited about being in your seminars.'

'Teaching was always my first love. But I liked being in Congress. It broke my heart to lose the election.'

'Will you go back to it?'

'Of course. This is just to keep me busy till I decide where to go from here. I'll probably end up in the Senate.'

'You sound very certain. I seem to recall the position is still elective.'

'I'm not certain, just confident. I can always teach, but right now I would be more valuable as a statesman.'

'The usual term is, politician. Why don't you run for mayor? It's available right now, since His Honour had that heart attack in the council chambers.'

'No, thanks. City government holds no fascination for me. I'm still deciding who to support in the special election to replace him.'

He was serious, she saw. Devon shrugged. Well, perhaps his endorsement of a candidate would be worth something. It and a half-dollar would buy a cup of coffee. 'You'd better decide soon.'

'That election is going to be a test of political power in the whole city. Whoever can win it could be a valuable ally two years from now, when I go after the Senate seat.'

'You're serious about that? You're already planning a campaign?'

He looked surprised that she had asked. 'Of course, but officially, I haven't decided what to do with myself. That's why I haven't signed a contract with the university yet.'

'But you do know you're going to run?'

'Sure.' He sipped his coffee, and then looked a bit alarmed. 'You aren't a reporter for the school paper in your spare time, are you?'

'No such luck,' Devon mocked. 'If you're going to be leaking stories, though, I'll see if I can scrape up some acquaintances. How does your wife feel about all this?'

'My wife? Oh, my wife.' He waved a hand. 'She doesn't care what I do, as long as I'm happy.'

'How very convenient for you,' Devon muttered. 'How old are your kids?'

'Twelve.'

She paused a moment, then put the cup down slowly. 'All three of them are twelve years old?'

'Yes. They're triplets. Didn't I tell you?'

'You know you didn't. Are they boys or girls?'

'Two boys and a girl. It's really very interesting medically, you see, because the boys are actually identical twins, and then the girl is a fraternal twin to . . .'

'I'm not listening to any more of this.' Devon

dumped the remains of her coffee down the drain. 'I think I'll go unpack.'

Roger was waiting for her at seven. He was sitting in the living room, feet propped up, outlining his view of the nation's economy to Jon, who was stretched out in the recliner, pipe in hand, listening patiently and putting in a comment here and there.

Devon stood in the doorway tapping her foot for a while, but as the minutes stretched out she gave up, took her coat off and sat down to read a magazine. Almost half an hour later Roger looked up. 'Aren't you ready yet, Dev?' he asked. 'We're going to be late to the game.'

Devon swore under her breath, but she put on her coat and said nothing at all until they were sitting in the battered station wagon.

'It isn't like you to be late, Devon,' Roger complained. 'You know how much I hate to miss the tip-off.'

'I wasn't late, Roger. You were so absorbed in Dr Hardesty's economics lecture that you didn't notice I was there.'

'It wasn't a lecture, it was fascinating. He can make the whole thing seem perfectly clear.'

'Most politicians can do that. It's what keeps them in office.'

'You don't need to make it sound like a dirty word, Dev. Jon's a nice guy.'

'I can't believe this! I am arguing with my date about whether my roommate is a nice guy!'

'I thought you had separate rooms.'

'We do. It was a figure of speech.'

Roger looked puzzled. 'If you don't like him, why are you living with him?'

They were at the auditorium by then. Devon swung her hair back over her shoulders and announced, 'Because I am part of a research experiment on how much mental anguish the human animal can stand.'

Roger's answer was lost in the roar of the crowd.

The apartment was nearly dark, but the back porch light was on. That was thoughtful of Jon, Devon thought as Roger parked the car near the back door. She yawned.

'I can take the hint,' Roger said.

'What hint?'

'The yawn. I'll come in some other time.'

'I'm genuinely tired from moving, Roger. Nothing more. If you'd like to come in for a while . . .'

'No. Get some sleep. I'll see you tomorrow.'

She raised an eyebrow, wondering why he was so certain he'd see her.

'Jon told me I could come over to watch the football game,' he explained. 'Brad's new girlfriend is in town, and he asked me to make myself scarce. I didn't want to miss the play-offs, so Jon said I could come here.'

'How kind of him.' It was his home; she could not argue with that. Jon could invite whomever he chose. But it looked to her as if he was doing his best to be aggravating.

Her stereo was playing a Bach suite, and Jon was dozing in his chair. A folder of lecture notes had spilled off his lap and was scattered over the floor; Cyan was curled up on his knee. When she saw Devon, the cat meowed loudly and stood up, stretching.

Jon opened his eyes and winced as the cat's claws dug ecstatically into his thigh. 'Was it a good game?'

'The home team won, but they had a difficult time of it. Were you waiting up for me?'

'Of course not.' He sounded offended. 'I was reviewing my lectures, and they put me to sleep. See what my students have to put up with?'

'If they are all as starry-eyed about you as Matt is, they won't even notice.' Devon bent to help him pick up the notes.

'If I'm lucky, it'll last a week or two. I really ought to reorganise all my lectures.'

'Why bother if you're only going to teach a semester?'

'Now is that any kind of attitude for a future teacher to have?'

Devon shrugged. 'Did I get any 'phone calls?'

'Have a heart. They just put in the 'phone this afternoon. Remember the fuss you put up to get them to install it on a weekend?'

'I forgot. A telephone is my lifeline, you see.'

'Well, it hasn't rung once. Maybe everyone realised that on Saturday night they weren't likely to find you at home.' He picked up the folders and stacked them neatly beside his chair. 'Are you as popular with the girls as you are with the men?'

'I have a lot of friends of both sexes. And I'm famous for my impromptu parties.'

'That sounds like a marvellous idea. I could meet some people . . .'

'I am not a social secretary, Jon. I don't know what kind of staff you had in Washington . . .'

'They didn't go in for impromptu.'

'Quit trying to manipulate me. It would be just as well, by the way, if you didn't answer the 'phone, because if Aunt Eleanor finds out I'm living with a man she'll be over here with a lynch mob.'

'Who is going to answer the 'phone, then? If Sylvia calls and you answer . . .'

'Sylvia?' Devon's tone was unbelieving. 'Is that your wife's name?' When he nodded solemnly, she went on, 'I thought you said you were going to explain it to her. And that she didn't care what you did, as long as you were happy.'

'There are limits to that attitude.'

'Ah. She's not as liberated a lady as she originally sounded. Of course, any woman who has three kids in a year . . .'

'You frown on that sort of thing?'

'I don't frown on babies; they'll provide me with a job twenty years from now. But the woman must have been a baby herself. It seems to me that you were rushing it.'

'I assure you, we didn't plan on having triplets.'

'I think you made the triplets up.'

Jon shrugged. 'That's an unusual way of phrasing it, but if standard English isn't good enough for you . . . How often do you have these little bashes?'

'About once a month in the past.'

'Good. They'll fit right in with my regular open house.'

'What?' Devon asked with foreboding.

'Long-standing practice. My students are invited to a bull session once a month.'

'Every month?'

'Of course. I like to get to know them outside the classroom too.'

Devon sighed. 'I think I'll give the parties up this semester.'

'Are you trying to hide me from your friends?'

'It's impossible to hide anything once Roger and Brad know it.'

'But you'd like to try, wouldn't you, Devon?'

She put her hands on her hips. 'Give me one reason why I should introduce you around. Look, it's difficult enough for an English major to get dates. Most guys won't ask me out at all because they think that I'll correct their grammar. The ones that do think I want to listen to their soupy poetry.'

'It doesn't look difficult for you to meet men,' Jon objected mildly.

'And now with you as an added handicap, I could go the whole semester without a date.'

'Accept it as a challenge,' he recommended. 'Why didn't you invite Roger in, by the way? I like him.'

'Roger is my friend, not yours.'

'Is he only allowed to have one friend?'

Devon stared at him. 'I am not going to argue with you. It is futile to exchange words with a politician.'

'Congratulations! You learned that in less than a day. It took Stella almost a year.'

'But you weren't a politician back then. Wait a minute! You said her name was Sylvia!'

'It is. Sylvia Stella Hardesty. Her friends call her S.S.'

'I hope she didn't lisp as a child,' Devon snapped.

He looked fascinated. 'I don't know. I'll have to ask her.'

'I am beginning to believe that not only are there no triplets, but there is no Stella Sylvia . . . whatever her name is . . . Hardesty either.'

'You have it turned around. And don't tell the triplets they don't exist. They'd be very angry at you.'

'I'll worry about that when I meet them. Are they going to be visiting you?'

'Not immediately. Their school is very demanding. And they're such perfectionists.'

Devon took that one with a grain of salt too. 'Are you planning to visit them?'

'Oh, no. Not until spring break, at least.'

'Don't you mind being an absent father?'

'Honey, you have no idea. I miss those little kids so.' He stood up and stretched lazily. 'I think I'll get some sleep. You mustn't let me bother you in the morning, by the way. I run five miles before breakfast every day.'

'As long as you don't do it in the apartment, I won't mind a bit,' Devon snapped.

She was careful to be quiet a few minutes later when she went upstairs. But there was only silence from the front bedroom.

'We're in for a long semester,' she told Cyan. The cat jumped up on the windowsill and meowed to be let out. 'It's too cold,' Devon told her. 'You like him, don't you, Cyan?' The cat just looked at her, then started to wash her face.

'To tell you the truth,' Devon murmured, brushing her hair, 'I can't help liking the scoundrel myself.'

CHAPTER THREE

DEVON'S eyes were still half-shut as she found her way down the stairs, tying the belt of her terry robe into a knot. She located Cyan's cat food in the cabinet and filled a bowl, making a mental note to buy a bigger dish so the darn cat wouldn't wake her up again. Then her nose led her to the coffeepot.

'There are some advantages to having a man around the house,' she muttered. Especially one who could make decent coffee. Perhaps, she decided, it wouldn't be so bad after all. They would both be busy with their classes, and Jon would soon find friends. They'd go their own directions. Devon sighed and filled her cup. At least, she hoped that was how it would work out.

She'd shared apartments before, and the arrangements had always been inconvenient. Usually it was a squabble over whose turn it was to cook or who had left the kitchen dirty that brought the relationship to an impasse. So Devon had learned to rent smaller apartments, ones she could afford by herself. She got lonely sometimes, she had to admit, but she could always invite her friends to visit. It wasn't possible to invite a roommate to leave.

In fact, she had to admit, splitting the rent on this apartment was the only thing that would keep her head above water. She had hoped that the money left from her job last summer would pay her living expenses this year. Every other semester, she had worked part time to supplement the small income that her mother's life insurance still provided. But she had hoped to enjoy this last year and concentrate on study instead of a job. However, her semester of practise teaching had cost her more than she had expected.

Now she would have to look for a part-time job again.

She and David were fortunate, at that; they didn't have to pay tuition costs. Their mother had worked for the university for years, and when she died a tuition-free education was one of the benefits left to them. Without it, neither of them would have had a prayer of attending any college at all, much less this expensive private university.

Just a few more months, Devon reflected, and she'd be earning her own living—if she could find a job. She could begin to make a settled life for herself. But for David and Julie that security was still years away. They were going to have a rough time of it, living with Aunt Eleanor. No, she'd done the right thing by refusing Julie's generous offer.

And since she and Jon were splitting the rent, she might even have room in her budget for a few extras. There were some clothes that she wanted, and after all, if she was going to be teaching next autumn, a new wardrobe was a necessity, not a luxury.

'Always assuming, of course, that you find a job,' she told herself. She reached for her handbag and checked the balance in her bank account. Well, there was no room there for luxuries just yet.

The telephone rang sharply, waking Cyan from her after-breakfast nap on the wide windowledge. Devon stared at it for three rings; should she answer it? On Sunday morning at ten it could be anyone. Finally she picked it up. If it was Sylvia—or Stella—or whatever the heck her name was—that was Jon's problem. He wasn't here to answer it.

It was Aunt Eleanor, and Devon breathed a sigh of relief that she had been the one to answer. Not that she really cared what Aunt Eleanor thought of her, she decided, but it was nice to keep a little peace in the family.

'Devon, darling,' Aunt Eleanor said, her voice syrupy sweet. 'Julie tells me you like your new apartment. Are you all settled in?'

'No, but I'm working on it. How did you get the number?'

'The nice young woman from directory assistance gave it to me. It's a good thing the telephone company provides the service. You probably wouldn't have remembered it till next weekend.' Her voice was cutting.

'I have been a bit busy, Aunt Eleanor.'

'Oh? Which one of your young men were you out with last night?' The question was probing.

It was certainly none of her aunt's business, but Devon knew that the woman would not rest till her question was answered. 'Roger took me to a basketball game.'

'Oh, yes. A likeable chap, though he seems a bit lacking in ambition.'

'Roger has plenty of ambition. He just isn't interested in the same things you are.'

'Perhaps you're right, Devon. All you young people seem to take interest in things no one else ever heard of. I thought by now there might be someone new. After all, you've been back in the city several days. But Julie said she had no idea.'

'Nobody that matters, Aunt Eleanor.' Sorry, Matt, she thought, but I am not willing to let Aunt Eleanor have that piece of information yet. Matt might turn out to be too important. And then of course there's Jon—but if Aunt Eleanor knew about Jon, she'd have a heart attack.

She pulled her thoughts back with a start. 'At least Julie and David are getting married,' Aunt Eleanor continued, and Devon wondered uneasily how much of the conversation she had missed. 'These young couples who don't bother with a ceremony before they begin to share a toothbrush . . .'

Devon could almost see her aunt's head shaking, and she shifted uneasily in her chair. Though of course, she told herself firmly, she and Jon were

hardly sharing a toothbrush. Or anything else more
intimate than a kitchen.

She was still irritated when she put the 'phone
down. Aunt Eleanor meant well, but she didn't
understand that Devon was grown up and responsible
for herself.

She sighed. It couldn't have been easy on Aunt
Eleanor, having Devon and David thrust on her when
their mother died. But then Eleanor hadn't made it
any easier.

She refilled her coffee cup. Never had she missed
her mother so much, she thought, remembering the
lovely, laughing woman who had kept them together
after their father had deserted them and never once
complained about how hard it was to feed and clothe
two fatherless teenagers. Her mother would have loved
Julie—the laughing warmth of her, and the dedication
that would make her a marvellous doctor. Devon's
mother would have understood.

The 'phone rang again, and this time Devon picked
it up without a thought. 'Hello?'

There was dead silence on the other end of the line.
Devon repeated herself, and finally got a faint reply.
'Is Jon Hardesty there?'

Oh, damn, Devon thought, and did the best
imitation of a secretary that she could muster. 'Not at
the moment, I'm afraid. Could I take a message?'

The voice was stronger now, as if the woman had
regained her self-possession. 'Tell him Mrs Hardesty
called. He has the number.'

I would hope he does, Devon told herself as she put
the 'phone down. She'd have sworn he was lying—the
whole story about Sylvia or Stella or whatever her
name was and the triplets . . . She sighed a little. Now
he'd have some explaining to do. 'And good enough
for him, too,' she told Cyan firmly. Cyan looked at her
thoughtfully and then, spotting a stray housefly that
had somehow survived the onset of winter, tried to bat
it down out of the window.

Jon came in the back door, red-faced from the cold, wearing a brown jogging suit. His eyes were bright and his hair was ruffled. 'I see Sleeping Beauty has awakened,' he announced cheerfully. 'Is breakfast ready?'

'I never eat it,' Devon said coolly.

Jon didn't seem to be crushed. 'I hope you didn't drink all the coffee.'

'Only two cups. There's plenty left for you.'

'I wouldn't count on it. It usually takes a whole pot to warm me up after five miles in this cold.'

'Speaking of being out in the cold—your wife called.'

'I told you that you shouldn't answer the 'phone.'

'We'd have had bigger trouble if you'd been here to answer the call before that. It was my Aunt Eleanor.'

'And she frowns on our arrangement?'

'She certainly would, if she knew about it.'

'I'll just pretend to be a new boyfriend,' he promised. He pulled the 'phone across the table.

'That might work in daylight hours, but what are we going to do when it rings at three in the morning?'

'Take it off the hook?' he suggested helpfully as he punched a string of numbers. 'I hate to interrupt this conversation, but I'd better call Stella back right away.'

'Doesn't she know you jog?'

'Sure. But usually I'm done with that by eight in the morning. Do you suppose if I told her I went to church . . .?'

'No,' Devon said firmly.

He waved a hand for silence and said into the phone, 'Hi, Jason. Is Mrs Hardesty in, please?'

'Is Jason one of the kids?' Devon murmured.

Jon put his hand over the mouthpiece. 'The middle one,' he whispered. 'Very formal. Never addresses his mother as anything but Mrs Hardesty—he thinks it's disrespectful to call her Mom.'

Devon didn't bother to answer that one. After all, she reminded herself, she'd asked for it.

'Hi, Stell,' Jon said. 'Sorry I was out. Yes, I know you said you'd call.' He made frantic motions towards his coffee cup, and Devon got up and refilled it for him. She pointed towards the cream and sugar, and he shook his head.

He was listening intently, forehead wrinkled. 'Stell, I'm shocked. How could you think such a thing of me?' He paused. 'I see. Well, news certainly travels fast, doesn't it?'

'Listening to one side of a conversation is crazy,' Devon announced under her breath, and she started for the living room.

Jon grinned, and as she left the room she heard him say, 'No, as a matter of fact it wasn't Margo who answered the 'phone. Does that make you feel better?'

Oh, God, Devon thought. Now she knows there are two of us! She shuddered and tried to hide herself in a book.

Jon came in a few minutes later and threw himself down in a chair. 'Stella is moderately upset,' he announced.

'Moderately upset? Is that what you call it?'

'I've seen her worse.'

'If she was closer, she'd murder you. And probably Margo and me, too.'

'If she was closer, I'd be worried,' he admitted. 'But the doctors think they have her straightened out now. As long as she takes her medicine, she doesn't hear those weird voices more than three or four times a day.'

Devon took a deep breath. This is all a hoax, she told herself. There is nothing to be upset about; it is all a fantasy.

He stood up, stretching like a cat. 'If you want to miss the best meal of the day, that's up to you,' he told her, 'but I'm going to fix breakfast. You're welcome to join me if you like.' He went to the kitchen without a backward glance.

Devon pulled her robe closer around her and held

her coffee mug between her hands. Perhaps, she thought, Jon was the one who was hearing weird voices. She made a mental note to do a bit of research. Just why had he lost that election?

The smell of bacon a few minutes later helped draw her back to the kitchen. He looked up from the pancake batter that he was pouring on to the griddle and smiled knowingly. Devon could have hit him with something. She refilled her cup with coffee she didn't want—just to have something to occupy her hands— and sat down at the kitchen table.

'Shouldn't we set some ground rules for the apartment?' she asked tentatively.

Jon shrugged. 'I suppose so. I'm pretty flexible, but there are a few things I object to. Tripping over my roommate and a guest making love on the living room floor is one of them.'

Devon's mouth dropped open. Finally, she said, with difficulty, 'I don't indulge myself on the living room floor.'

'Good. All intimate guests will go to the bedrooms, then.'

'Wait a minute! What's your definition of an intimate guest? I don't plan to take every man I bring home to my bedroom.'

Those big brown eyes summed her up. 'An intimate guest is one whose actions make an audience uncomfortable. Got it?'

'I do not entertain in my bedroom,' Devon said flatly.

Jon put the pancake turner down and leaned against the counter top. 'Are you a virgin, Devon?'

She stared at him. 'By what possible stretch of the imagination is it any of your business?'

'I just like to know what to expect from my roommates. If I'm going to be running into another man in the bathroom, I like to know it ahead of time— it's only good manners to leave me a note or something.'

Devon stood up. 'There is obviously no point in discussing anything with you,' she said, holding on to her dignity.

Jon shrugged and piled pancakes on to his plate. 'I believe in telling things as they are.'

She heard a car pull up to the back door, and peeked out the window. 'It's Roger,' she groaned.

Jon glanced at his watch. 'He's a little early—I forgot to mention that he's watching the game with me.'

'He told me.' Devon ran a hand over her hair and started for the stairs.

He looked puzzled. 'Why are you getting so bent out of shape?'

She paused on the second step. 'I can't let him see me like this!'

Jon lifted the strips of bacon out of the pan and laid them out to drain. 'I hate to be the one who points this out, Devon, but you've looked like that all morning and no one has screamed and run away. Or threatened to attack you, either.'

Devon hadn't thought of that. She looked down at the terry robe and wondered why she hadn't felt self-conscious with Jon around. 'You don't count.'

'Obviously Roger does. And just as obviously, you've never slept with him, or you wouldn't mind him seeing you in a bathrobe.' He looked her over thoughtfully. 'You actually are a virgin, aren't you?'

'I suppose you didn't know there were any left in the college community.'

Jon shrugged and pushed Cyan's nose away from the plate of bacon. 'I think a roommate should know these things. It prevents a lot of discomfort. Of course, there is an age beyond which virginity should not be perpetuated,' he said thoughtfully. 'It gets in everyone's way.' He opened the back door. 'Good morning, Roger.'

Devon made as graceful a retreat as possible up the stairs to the shower. It took a long time under the hot spray before her anger simmered down, but she finally decided that showing her irritation to Jon was certain to make him continue the hazing. Perhaps if she ignored him altogether, he'd decide that teasing her was no fun.

She dressed in soft, faded jeans and a ski sweater, and pulled her hair back with a ribbon. If Jon and Roger were going to watch a playoff game, she would go out for the afternoon. She certainly was in no mood to watch two squads of football players try to commit mass homicide.

Roger was ensconced at the kitchen table, gesturing with his fork as he consumed pancakes and bacon. Jon poured another cupful of batter on to the griddle as Devon came down the stairs. 'Are you certain you don't want breakfast, Devon?' he asked.

'I told you, I never eat breakfast.'

'You're missing a great meal, Dev,' Roger announced.

'I won't object if you want to call it lunch. It's late enough.' Jon flipped the pancakes over; he had obviously practised the skill.

'No, thanks. I'm going over to the library for a while.'

He looked her over from head to foot. 'You just don't want to be obligated to cook tonight.'

'That's one good reason. Enjoy the game.'

'I will tell your adoring public where you've gone. I hope not many of them call.'

The cold fresh air slapped against her face as she crossed the campus, which lay almost deserted under the fresh blanket of snow. With classes not yet in session, most students were still settling back into dorm rooms or apartments and celebrating the last day of freedom of the Christmas break. Only a few were already hitting the books.

'Devon!' The shout seemed to come from halfway across campus.

She looked around and waved when she spotted Matt almost half a block away. He broke into a trot.

'No need to run,' she told him when he came up beside her, puffing in the crisp air. 'I'm in no hurry.' His blond head was bare, but he wore bright blue earmuffs. They almost matched his eyes, Devon thought. He was the most magnificently handsome man she had ever met.

'Going to the library?' he asked.

'Yes. Not to study, though. I thought I'd pick up a novel to while away a boring Sunday afternoon.'

'In that case, let's avoid boredom together. I tried to call you, but your friend said you'd moved and didn't have a 'phone yet.'

'Julie's behind the times. I'll give you the number.'

Matt rubbed his hands together and blew on them. 'Your pen will freeze if you try to use it out here. Let's go someplace where it's warm. Your apartment, maybe?'

'I still want to get a book.'

Matt grinned. 'I think I can stand the library's atmosphere that long. I'll read the Sunday paper.'

The big brick library with its high-arched windows was tomb-silent. Devon checked the shelves of new books and picked up the latest novel by her favourite author. It would entertain her for the evening, at least, she thought. She checked it out and turned towards the reference section, where Matt had spread out the big Sunday edition of the newspaper.

Devon pulled out a chair across from him and picked up the book review section. Matt was deeply absorbed in the editorial page. The occasional muted ringing of a telephone was the only interruption, and even that was rare today.

None of the reviews caught her fancy, so she reached for her novel. Then her eyes fell on the latest large, red-bound volume of *Who's Who in America*, on the shelf behind Matt's left shoulder.

She tried to tell herself that it didn't matter whether Jon was telling the truth, but her fingers seemed to have a mind of their own, pulling the book off the shelf and flipping through the flimsy sheets, searching

down the columns of names till she found
HARDESTY, Jonathan Dexter: Member, United
States Congress.

A quick bit of arithmetic told her he was thirty-two.
'Just a little young to have twelve-year-old kids,' she
muttered under her breath. Born in Chicago, Illinois,
son of Seth and Stella Dexter Hardesty—Devon
sniffed. So it was his mother who had been shocked
this morning when a woman answered Jon's telephone,
she thought. That certainly explained a lot.

And not only didn't he have three kids, but
according to *Who's Who*, he'd never been married.

Devon ignored the rest—the colleges he'd attended,
the ones he'd taught at, his political party and
philosophy—and slammed the book shut. 'Talk about
gullible,' she muttered. 'He had you half-believing all
that nonsense.'

Matt turned around, eyebrows raised. 'Did you say
something, Devon?'

Even the reference librarian, bending over a book at
the next table, looked up in surprise. 'Can I help you,
Miss?'

Devon hadn't even noticed the woman. 'Oh—no,
thanks. It was nothing.' She pushed *Who's Who* back
on to the shelf and picked up her novel, red-cheeked
with embarrassment. It's bad enough to talk to
yourself, she thought in aggravation as she sat down
again, but to do it in a library . . .

Matt gave her a questioning look, but he soon
retreated into his newspaper again. Devon glanced at
the article he was reading. It took up most of a page,
and the headline read, 'Is the Statehouse in Jon
Hardesty's Future?'

Matt caught her glance. 'Want to read it?'

Devon shook her head. She thought about saying, I
already know more about the gentleman's future than
the newspaper does.

'Fascinating man,' Matt said, and pushed the paper
aside.

'Is he some kind of hero of yours?' Devon asked
tartly. 'And what did he ever do to win that kind of
respect?'

'I don't agree with him on every stand, but that's
the main thing about Jon Hardesty that attracts
attention. He does his research, he makes up his mind,
and he sticks to his opinion. No dancing around an
issue or letting every side believe that he agrees with
them.' Matt sighed. 'He plays politics when he has to,
but not on issues that are important to him.'

'Why is everybody speculating on what he's going
to do?' Devon propped her elbows on the table and
rested her chin on her folded hands. 'After all, he was
defeated. What does it matter what he does now?'

Matt grinned. 'It's obvious you're no politician.
That election was a fluke, and the man who took
Hardesty's Congressional seat is already running
scared of what will happen two years from now.'

'What do you think he's going to do?'

'The Senate,' Matt said instantly. 'But I don't think
he'll stay out of public life for two years. I'll bet that
come next summer he's back in Washington. There
are still a few powerful members of his party—Bob
Dickinson for one. Hardesty will have a government
appointment before the year is out.'

'But you don't think he'd run for governor?'

'No chance. Whoever wrote that article hasn't given
it much thought. Being Governor would be a waste of
time for Jon Hardesty; the power isn't in the state
capitol.' Matt scrambled the newspaper back into a
pile and returned it to the shelf. 'Let's go over to the
Student Union, if you're finished here.'

His smile was blindingly attractive; men like Matt
Lyon didn't come into a girl's life every day. Devon's
heart melted. She nodded, and thought, I believe I'd
go anywhere with you, Matt.

CHAPTER FOUR

DEVON pulled open the heavy glass door of the liberal arts building and stopped to glance at her watch. She had half an hour till her class in modern history; she hoped her adviser wasn't busy this afternoon.

She ran up the steps to the office floor. The building was just a year old, but already it was overflowing and liberal arts classes were again being held in every cranny the department could find across campus. But Devon was lucky this semester; most of her classes were in the new building.

Dr Driscoll was in his office. Devon paused in the doorway, and he looked up from the stack of papers to study her over half-glasses. 'Devon Quinn, as I live and breathe. I thought you'd transferred to the state university or done some other idiotic thing.'

'I've only been back for two weeks, Doc,' Devon protested mildly.

'But if you're going to graduate this spring, we have to get started, my dear. Come in, come in. Sit down.'

Devon glanced around the office. Every flat surface was filled with books, folders, newspapers. 'Where?' she asked.

'Oh. Just slide those things on to the floor.'

She did. 'What do we have to start on?'

'Getting you a job, for one thing. I assume you still plan to work?'

'Do I have other choices?'

He shook his head sadly. 'I still think you should stay for graduate school, Devon.'

She looked at him with mild resentment. 'Why didn't you tell me four years ago that an English teacher needs a master's degree? Now it's too late.'

Doc pushed his chair back and propped his feet on

the corner of his desk. Two books and a research paper cascaded on to the floor, but Doc didn't seem to notice. 'It's never too late. You'll be cutting it close by applying now, but you can still do it.'

'My grades just aren't good enough, Doc. Remember? The graduate school would laugh at me.'

'Have you tried?' When Devon didn't answer, he continued, 'It would only take one more year, Devon, and the master's degree would mean all the difference when you start looking for a position.'

'I can't afford it, Doc.'

'You could easily get a teaching fellowship. You can teach freshman English and earn your living expenses.'

Devon shook her head.

Driscoll sighed. 'Well, at least take this home and look it over. It's the graduate school packet, and if you'd just look at it, you'll find that it isn't so impossible after all.'

'I'll look, but I make no further promises,' Devon said. 'I'd better go. I don't dare be late to Modern Problems. And speaking of that class—it is a modern problem by itself. Why did you sign me up for it?'

'I didn't. I just agreed to it. Remember? You wanted it because it's the only history class that fits your schedule, and you needed the hours. Just as you're taking dancing because you need the physical education hours.'

'I'll never understand how you keep all these schedules in your head, Doc.'

'I have to. If I write it down, I can never find the slip of paper again.' He gestured around at the confusion with a grin. 'Besides, I wanted to see how good it was.'

'Introductory dance? I'm hardly a fair critic.'

'No. Modern Problems.'

'Oh, that.' Devon wrinkled her nose distastefully. 'Thanks for making me a guinea pig. So far, it isn't worth the time.'

'Who teaches it?'

'Dr Burton. He's dry and boring and dull, and most of the people in the class are political science majors. They may enjoy him, but I feel very out of place.'

'Well, you should have a nice change today. Burton's in the hospital.'

'What happened?'

'He had surgery last night for appendicitis. Enjoy your holiday, Devon.' Doc pulled his chair back up to the desk.

Devon paused at the office door. 'Oh, Doc? If you hear of anyone needing tutoring . . .'

'Need to pick up a few dollars?'

'Quite a few.'

He looked at her thoughtfully over the thick lenses of his half-glasses. 'Want to take on a book?'

'From scratch? Or do you mean editing?'

'Probably a ghost-writing job from the man's first draft. I haven't seen it.'

'Sure. I'll look at it, at least.'

Doc grunted. 'I'll give Hardesty your name.'

'Who?' Devon asked with foreboding.

'Jon Hardesty. He's a new staff member.'

'I know that much. He's writing a book?'

'Yeah. His experiences in federal government, I think. Or maybe it's an analysis of Washington women he has known.' He winked and leered.

'I'll bet that would fill a book,' Devon muttered.

'It might offend your Puritan conscience, Devon. Politics isn't always pretty.'

'If there's money in it, I'll chance it. See you later, Doc.'

The early winter dark was hovering over the campus; the wrought iron lamps that bordered the asphalted paths were flickering on one by one. Devon hesitated in the door of the lecture hall. If Dr Burton wasn't going to hold class, someone would have put a notice on the blackboard. But the board was bare, and scattered around the room were students already in their seats. Most of them were boning up on today's reading assignment.

Devon wondered if Doc had, for once, got his facts mixed up. She dropped into a seat in the back of the hall and started to doodle on a fresh sheet in her notebook. At least she'd see Matt; the only good thing about the class had been discovering that Matt was taking it too.

He was in the seat beside her before she heard him come in. 'Why are you sitting here?' he questioned. 'Old Burton isn't going to show up. Let's cut out for a beer.'

Devon glanced at her watch. 'I think I'll stick around. If class was cancelled, there'd be a notice posted.'

'What could he do? Make a tape of his lecture and send his secretary to play it?'

'I've heard of crazier things, so I'm going to sit here for a while, just in case they take attendance. He lowers grades for cutting classes, you know.'

Matt scoffed. 'Devon, don't be a chicken. It's your last semester. I'm not going to waste my afternoon here.' He stood up, all six feet of elegant grace. 'Tell you what—I'm going to the Union tonight. Come on over when you're finished here.'

'Maybe.'

'Come on, Devon. Be a sport.' He stopped in the doorway to talk to a brown-haired co-ed. That dreamy smile flashed again and the co-ed fluttered her eyelashes. Then they walked out together.

Devon shrugged. She had no strings on him, that was for certain. They'd had only one official date, the symphony concert. She wondered if she looked as silly when Matt smiled at her as that co-ed had. She fervently hoped not.

There was a stir at the front of the room. She turned around in her seat to see Jon leaning on the desk. A flicker of interest ran through the students.

'I'm Jon Hardesty,' he said. 'I'm guest-starring today for Dr Burton. I'm sure you've all heard about his misfortune by now, so I won't go into detail, except to point out that when one is past the first flush of youth . . .'

Appreciative laughter rippled through the room. Dr Burton was nearly seventy.

'. . . even minor surgery is no longer minor. Dr Burton will be gone at least six weeks.'

Students' faces began to reflect concern. Many of them were seniors, and this course was required for their graduation.

'The department is offering you several options. You can drop the class without penalty, you can see your adviser and transfer into another course, or you can stick around and watch me pinch hit.'

'Just my luck,' Devon muttered.

'I need to warn you, however,' Jon continued, 'that I am not another Dr Burton.'

'Good,' said a deep male voice in the back of the room. 'I'll stay.'

Jon smiled. 'I'll pretend I didn't hear that,' he promised. His eyes, roaming the room, rested thoughtfully on Devon. He raised an eyebrow, but gave no other sign of recognition.

A co-ed in the front row raised her hand. 'What about assignments? Will you follow Dr Burton's outline?'

'I think I can manage my own,' Jon told her gravely. 'You can plan on reading fewer textbooks and more newspapers.'

'I bought all these books for no reason?' the co-ed wailed.

'You can use them as doorstops,' Jon suggested helpfully. 'For the next class meeting I want a list from each of you—what you think are the ten most serious problems facing this nation today. See you next Tuesday. Class dismissed.'

Devon stacked her books and slowly stood up. Too bad Matt hadn't stuck around; he would have been delighted that his idol was taking over the class. \

She stopped at the corner drugstore to get a quart of milk. Late afternoon classes were the worst, she concluded as she walked home in the rapidly gathering dark. She really didn't mind the early ones, but she liked to be home where it was light and warm before the dusk settled in. Light and warmth and something savoury simmering on the stove—she'd make spaghetti tonight, she decided. A heavy, rich tomato sauce over steaming pasta . . . She'd even be generous and see if Jon wanted to join her.

'He'll probably think I'm trying to bribe the teacher,' she muttered.

The ten biggest problems facing the country, she thought. Jon was biting off a lot, to turn Dr Burton's class into a discussion group. But that seemed to be what he intended. She shrugged; it was his business, after all. And it was certain to be more interesting than Burton's lectures.

Cyan was under the kitchen table, her eyes blood-red as they reflected the light. She was chewing on a large, soft, dark lump. Devon sighed. 'Cyan, what have you got now?'

Jon called from upstairs, 'Is that you, Devon?'

'No, it's Lizzie Borden. What are you going to do about it?'

'I didn't know you were taking Burton's class.'

'If I'd known he was going to get sick, I'd have warned you. Can I have the kitchen?'

'Depends on where you're going to take it.' His head appeared around the corner of the stairs. He was towelling his hair briskly. 'As a matter of fact, you can have the whole place to yourself tonight. I'm going out.'

'Oh.' Devon's voice was small.

Jon's eyebrows went up and he padded down the stairs in terry robe and slippers. 'You sound disappointed. Or am I imagining things?'

'I was going to make spaghetti sauce. It seems a waste to do it just for me.'

'It sounds good, too. A lot better than what I'll be eating tonight. Sometimes I think if I never again see a pile of green beans with almonds it will be too soon.'

'If you don't like it . . .'

'Why eat it? A good question, my dear. It's a political party function, and the menus never vary.'

'Never?'

'Rarely,' he amended. 'That's how I keep my boyish figure. It's either soggy fried chicken or cold roast beef—but it's always green beans with almonds. They taste like alfalfa. Tell you what,' he persuaded, 'if you'll wait till tomorrow on the spaghetti, I'll make the sauce.'

'I like making sauce,' Devon protested.

He smiled down into her eyes and flicked her cheek with a careless finger. 'All right. I'll make the spaghetti. I'm not choosy.'

He went back upstairs to get dressed, and a moment later Devon jumped a foot as he bellowed, 'Where the hell did my socks go?'

Cyan, eyes bright, retreated a little farther under the table. Devon looked at her suspiciously and bent to retrieve the dark lump on which the cat had been chewing.

She carried the folded socks upstairs and tapped on Jon's door. 'Are you looking for these?'

'Where did you find them?' He took the bundle out of her hand. 'They're wet,' he accused.

'Cyan thought you'd given her a new toy.'

'I'm going to kill that cat. Wait and see.' He tossed the socks towards the dresser, and Cyan, who had followed Devon upstairs, pounced on them again.

Devon decided that retreat was an excellent idea. She changed into the black leotard and tights that was the standard uniform for her dance class. 'Waiting till the last semester to take a required class wasn't brilliant, Quinn,' she told herself. Dance was the only class that had fit her schedule, and choreographing a routine to a Broadway show number was not going to be one of her favourite pastimes. She put a record on the stereo and tried out a few of the steps the instructor had showed them.

She had no idea how long Jon had been standing in the doorway watching, but when she made a particularly clumsy turn and lost her balance, he of course was there to see it. He seemed to be gritting his teeth.

'If it looks so easy, why don't you try it?' she challenged.

'I wasn't thinking that it looked easy,' he denied. 'In fact, it was another adjective altogether.'

'Clumsy?' Devon collapsed on to the couch. 'That's what the instructor will probably say.'

'No. Sexy was the word I had in mind. You really do a number on my pulse rate in that outfit, you know. I'm not exactly a doddering grandfather.'

She tried to look casual as she pulled an afghan off the back of the couch and wrapped it around her.

Jon laughed, but there was a disturbing warmth in his eyes as he studied every inch that wasn't covered by the afghan.

Devon raised her chin defiantly and stared back at him. She didn't know what she had expected, but he took her by surprise. His dark brown tuxedo was tailored to perfection, the neutral beige shirt pleated to show off gold studs and cufflinks. Nothing too elaborate or fancy, just restrained good taste, she thought, and wondered if his mother had chosen the set. He wasn't handsome, strictly speaking, she thought, but—he was strikingly good looking.

'Will I pass inspection?' he teased.

She remembered the day they had met, and how he had asked, after she had looked him over, if she liked what she saw. He needed to be taken down a peg, she thought. 'You'll do,' she said coolly.

His eyes sparkled. 'Is that the best you can do, Dev?' he wheedled.

'Except for the cat hair,' she added and removed

one of Cyan's cream-coloured hairs from his velvet lapel.

'Whenever Sox decides to run away from home, she can count on my help.' He pulled a topcoat from the closet. 'If Stella should happen to call . . .'

Devon said sweetly, 'I will tell her that her son has gone out to dinner.'

Jon raised an eyebrow. 'Been doing your research? If Margo calls, tell her I'm on my way.'

'Great,' Devon muttered. 'If I can't find a teaching job, I'll just start an answering service.'

'It wouldn't be profitable,' Jon retorted from the door. 'Nine out of ten calls around here are for you.'

Margo didn't call, but Matt did, a couple of hours later. Devon untangled the sleeping cat from her lap so she could reach the 'phone, and remembered abruptly that she had been invited to join him at the Student Union.

'Sorry I didn't come over, Matt,' she said.

'That's all right. Why don't you come over now? We'll work on Hardesty's idea of Modern Problems homework.' Matt sounded frustrated.

'I thought he was your hero.'

'I'd already read all of Burton's assignments, clear through midterm.'

'And then Dr Hardesty changes the rules,' Devon commiserated. She looked at the clock and remembered that she hadn't eaten. 'Sure, I'll come over and get a sandwich and we can talk about the assignment.'

'I'll be here.'

He was waiting in the warm lobby of the Student Union, leaning against a panelled wall, arms crossed. He was so handsome, his blond hair striking against a robin's egg blue sweater. He looked up and smiled when she came in, and Devon's heart melted.

Never, she thought, never have I felt this way about a man. Matt was a special, sensitive, wonderful person. I'll have to introduce him to Julie and David, she thought.

Matt came across to her and gave her a possessive kiss, and Devon forgot that she disliked being kissed in public places.

'I had a better idea,' he said, draping an arm about her shoulders. 'It's getting dull around here. Let's walk over to my place—there's a good movie on television.'

'I haven't eaten yet. And what about the assignment?'

He smiled again, white teeth flashing. 'I have food. And we'll talk about the problems of the nation during the commercials.'

He picked up his coat, and Devon was out the door before she had a chance to protest. Not that she objected exactly, she decided, but she didn't make a habit of visiting a man's apartment.

What nonsense, Devon, she told herself crossly, to be uneasy with Matt.

Matt's apartment was an efficiency, with a tiny kitchen in one end of the big room and a neatly arranged living room in the other. The studio bed was folded up to make a couch.

'Take your shoes off,' Matt recommended. 'The snow will soak through and get your feet wet.'

Devon kicked her shoes off and gave him her coat. 'The apartment's cute,' she said.

He waved a hand around the room. 'It's little, but it's all mine,' he announced. 'Which reminds me, I have to start getting close to that roommate of yours.'

He certainly sounded calm about it, Devon thought. She hadn't mentioned Jon to him—who could have? How did he know about Jon? 'Roommate?' she asked uneasily.

Matt smiled. 'Obviously you have one, or you'd have invited me over before now.'

Well, he was right on target with that one, Devon thought.

Matt turned on the television. 'A little charm is all

that's required. A couple of days and I'll have her eating out of my hand. Roommates in general are a pain in the neck, you know.'

'I know,' Devon said. 'I haven't had one for a while.' Now was the time to tell him, she thought. Matt would understand. Everyone in the college community understood the crazy things that students did because they lacked money. Sharing an apartment with a man was nothing compared to the stunts some girls pulled.

He sat down on the couch and patted the seat beside him. Devon took it reluctantly. 'I got tired of hanging a necktie on the door when I wanted to entertain,' he said, 'so I got a place of my own. Now when a lady wants to stay the night, nobody gets mad.' He stretched lazily and put an arm around her shoulders.

Devon shifted uneasily under his arm, and then settled down to watch the movie. Perhaps she was a coward, she told herself, but she was uncomfortable discussing the subject. You're a moralistic old hen, she scolded herself. She shouldn't be bothered by the idea that there had been other women in Matt's life. It certainly came as no surprise; nobody lived like a monk these days.

Except you, Devon, she told herself. Then she tried to laugh it off. Just because everyone else seemed to be sleeping around didn't mean that she had to feel out of place. There were still men—somewhere—who appreciated old-fashioned fidelity. Someday she would meet a man she could trust—one who would be as true to her as she was prepared to be to him. She just hadn't run into any for a while. Even Jon had been amazed that a twenty-two-year-old virgin was still to be found. What was it he had said—something about there being an age when virginity began to get in everyone's way. She smiled. Jon did have a way of putting things . . .

'What's the joke?' Matt asked.

'Oh—nothing.'

He smiled, but didn't press the subject. A few

minutes later, he said, 'The movie stinks.'

Devon, who had been enjoying it, didn't protest. He turned the television to another channel and came back to sit beside her. 'So how are we going to entertain ourselves?' he asked softly.

'What about the assignment?'

Matt shrugged. 'Next week,' he said, and kissed her.

Devon wouldn't have been human if she hadn't enjoyed that kiss, but when he pushed her down on the couch, his weight holding her still, she protested.

Matt grinned and teased, 'What's the matter, Devon? That old game—you argue, and I persuade? Let's not waste time. You knew when you came that I wanted to make love to you. Let's stop playing games and enjoy each other.'

'It's not a game,' she protested. 'I don't want this.'

'Sure you do. It's all right to enjoy it, Devon. I won't think less of you.'

Did she want Matt to make love to her? Was that why she had come, unconsciously knowing what would happen? No, she told herself. Making love was for people who cared deeply about each other, not a game for those who were only beginning to get acquainted.

But during her moments of questioning, his hands were busy under her sweater, and Devon gasped as he unfastened her bra. 'That good little girl pose of yours gets tiresome,' Matt said, his lips against her throat.

'Stop it, Matt! I don't want you to do this!'

He pulled back for a moment, eyes narrowed. Suddenly he wasn't handsome anymore. 'Are you telling me that you don't want to make love, or that you don't want me?'

'Either.' Talk about euphemisms, she thought, her brain running at lightning speed. This wasn't making love, this was rape, pure and simple.

'We'll see about that,' Matt said curtly. 'You asked for this, Devon. You came here willingly. And now you're trying to back out.'

Devon winced as his caresses became rougher, and for the first time she really understood what was happening. And there would be no help from anyone; no one knew where she was.

She considered bursting into tears, but she didn't think that would stop him. She gulped and said, 'Matt—please. It really is the first time. Just give me a few minutes.'

He looked at her suspiciously, and she stared back, forcing her expression to be innocent, friendly, willing. 'I have to use the bathroom,' she murmured.

He laughed, then. 'All right, little one,' he said and patted her cheek. 'I'll be waiting. Eagerly.'

The bathroom door didn't lock. She stood, leaning against the sink, for as long as she dared, trying to drown her fear so that her mind could function again. If she could just get out of the apartment, she thought, she could run for it.

She looked down at the heavy socks on her feet and cursed the snow on the ground and her own innocence in kicking off her shoes as Matt had suggested. And her coat was in the closet, where he had so carefully hung it up.

Coats and shoes don't matter, Devon, she told herself firmly. If there was no time to retrieve them, she'd leave them behind. If, she thought grimly, she had a chance to run.

She turned the water on, wondering just how long she could pretend to be washing her hands.

The door opened behind her. 'Come on, honey. I can't wait forever, you know.'

'Just a minute,' she said over her shoulder.

He came up behind her, and his hands insinuated themselves over her shoulders and down to cup her breasts. Devon's reaction was instinctive. With every ounce of strength she possessed, she drove an elbow back into his chest, striking him firmly right below the ribs.

It caught him off balance and he went down, sprawling heavily on to the tile floor. 'Why, you little . . .' he sputtered.

Devon didn't wait around for his assessment of her character. She fled through the apartment, lost precious moments fumbling at the unfamiliar lock, then was down the stairs and out on to the street, the sound of Matt's pursuit echoing in her ears.

The cold blast of winter air hit her like a truck. She pulled up for an instant to survey her situation. Eleven blocks from home, no shoes, no coat—did she have her apartment key or had she put it in her coat pocket?

There was no time to look for it. She pulled open the door of the dark little tavern on the corner and went in.

The row of men at the bar turned and looked at her curiously. The bartender looked her over and said, 'You can't come in here without shoes.'

Devon snapped, 'Look, if I had my shoes I wouldn't need to be here. All I want to do is use the 'phone.'

'Pay 'phone on the back wall,' he grunted and turned back to his work.

It was a booth. She searched the pockets of her jeans grimly, hoping that she didn't have to beg for change, and found two dimes. Thanking heaven that at least her call would be private, she sank on to the bench and dropped the dimes into the phone.

The number rang forever, it seemed to Devon, before the receiver was picked up. 'Devon Quinn's answering service,' said a firm baritone.

'Jon?' It came out as a croak, and Devon had to try again. 'I need help. Will you come and get me?'

'What happened?'

'My date tried to—Oh, my God, he's here.'

'Where the hell is "here"?' Jon sounded frustrated.

Devon gave him the address. 'Hurry. Please hurry. Oh, and bring me some shoes.'

'I'll be there in two minutes. In the meantime, call the police.'

'I can't. I don't have any more dimes.'

'So you called me first? I'm touched by your faith in me. Pretend that you're talking to the police, Devon.'

Matt had stopped at the bar, and when he finally walked back to the phone booth he was carrying a mug of beer. He looked relaxed and at ease.

Devon wondered if he did this sort of thing often. She propped her feet against the door of the booth so it couldn't be opened and held the phone to her ear.

'Devon. You're not doing anything stupid like calling the cops, are you?' Matt asked quietly. 'Because if you are, I'll tell the truth. You came willingly to my apartment, you led me on, and then when I did what you indicated you wanted, you hit me.'

Devon didn't dignify that with an answer. He was still standing there, pleading with her to come out and talk to him, when Jon opened the front door. It had been very little longer than two minutes. It felt like two years to Devon.

He's not wearing the tuxedo, she thought irrelevantly. He must have been home for a while when I called.

Jon's face seemed to relax when he saw her. Then he, too, walked up to the bar and ordered a drink. Devon could have screamed in frustration. Just get me out of here, Jon, she wanted to shout.

Jon stirred his Scotch and water, put the swizzle stick aside, and came back to the booth. On his face was an expression of polite interest. 'Mr Lyon? I thought I recognised you. And Miss Quinn.'

Devon hung up the phone and opened the door. She was still shaking.

Jon seemed to notice for the first time that her feet were shoeless, wet, and twisting together in nervous anxiety. 'Have you had an accident, Miss Quinn?' he asked politely. 'I'd be happy to give you a ride home.'

The expression in his eyes demanded that she play along. Devon shakily said, 'Thank you, Dr Hardesty. Matt—if you would get my coat and shoes . . .'

'That would be very kind of you, Mr Lyon. My car is out front, if it isn't too much trouble to bring them there.'

Matt hadn't said a word. He shook his head as if to clear confusion away, set the beer down and walked out the front door.

'I wonder if we'll get the—coat and shoes both, did you say? Devon, you are so careless with your things.' Jon pulled her on to her feet.

She was shivering. 'He'll bring them. He's afraid of you.'

'Is that why you called me? I could have done without the honour.' He looked thoughtfully at the mixed drink in his hand and then set it, untouched, on the bar. At the door he looked from her feet to the little green sports car, which was parked carelessly by a fireplug, engine running. 'Sorry, I didn't think I should waste time looking for shoes.'

'I can walk.' But Devon didn't sound convinced.

He didn't argue. He just picked her up and carried her to the little car. He put her into the passenger seat, and Devon stretched her feet out gratefully in the stream of warm air from the heater.

'I wish that you had hit him,' she said when Jon slid behind the wheel.

'What would that have accomplished? Why did you call me instead of your brother, by the way?'

'David would have killed him,' Devon admitted.

Jon shrugged. 'I see violence runs in the family. Preserving the status quo works much better. This way he doesn't know for certain how much you've told me—which isn't much, by the way.'

She told him briefly what had happened. By the time she'd finished, Matt was coming towards the car, her coat and shoes in his hand.

'I'll be damned,' Jon said. He got out of the car and handed the items in to Devon. She couldn't hear all of the conversation as she slid the shoes on over her soggy socks. But she could hear the tone of voice, and Jon didn't sound angry or upset or threatening.

'Sorry you didn't get to enjoy your drink,' she said when Jon got back into the car.

'Pure camouflage,' he admitted. 'Besides, I saw the label on the bottle. It was nothing they'd drink in Edinburgh, believe me.'

The ride home was quiet. 'I still wish you'd have hit him,' Devon admitted as Jon parked the car at the back door.

'Bloodthirsty, aren't you?'

'Do you think I should file charges or something?'

'No.'

She waited for more, but Jon didn't add a word. She followed him into the living room, where Cyan woke up, stretched, meowed, and jumped into Jon's arms.

'Why not?' she asked. 'Don't you believe me?'

'Of course,' he said, surprised. He scratched the cat's chin and added, 'I also believe that more rapes occur on dates than in any other way. But you did go willingly to his apartment, and you were not actually assaulted. You couldn't prove a thing.' Then his eyes hardened. 'Damn it, Devon, don't you have any more sense than that?' His voice was tightly controlled, but his anger was obvious. 'When I think of what could have happened to you ... It makes me want to beat you myself!'

Tears ran silently down her cheeks. Jon put a gentle arm around her shoulders, and she buried her face in his shoulder, sobbing.

He put the protesting cat on the floor and sat down, pulling Devon down beside him. He held her for a long time, letting her cry out the fear and the hurt and the disillusionment. At last she lay quiet in his arms, vaguely aware of the soft sweater under her cheek and the scent of his pipe tobacco tickling her nose.

He stroked her hair with a gentle hand. 'Don't go to sleep on me, Devon,' he warned.

'I'm not sleepy,' she said, and yawned. 'You would

never do that to a girl, would you,' she asked, but it
wasn't a question.

'Don't put it past any man. You're too trusting.'

'But you wouldn't.'

'Well—if I tried it, she wouldn't run out into the
snow minus coat and shoes, that's sure. Matt's
technique is a little abrupt. Have a hot bath, Devon.
You'll feel better.'

She opened her eyes and let them close again. 'I'm
too comfortable to move.'

'If you go to sleep and I have to carry you upstairs,'
he threatened, 'you might find yourself in my bed
instead of your own.'

She sat up straight. 'Men!' she stormed. 'You're all
alike!'

'That, my dear, is exactly what I've been trying to
tell you.' He reached for his pipe and the evening
newspaper. 'Good night, Devon. If you have a
nightmare—don't call for me.'

CHAPTER FIVE

DEVON was humming a tune as she came down the street. A good night's sleep had restored her sense of humour, and she was looking forward to spaghetti.

The landlady was at the kerb, emptying a wastebasket into the dustbin. She greeted Devon cheerfully, and said, 'That handsome husband of yours is already home.'

Husband? Devon was still reeling from that comment when the landlady added another.

'Good-looking as he is, I don't know why you let him out of your sight. Plenty of girls out there just waiting for a man, Mrs Hardesty. Especially those college girls.'

'My name isn't Hardesty—it's Quinn,' Devon managed to say.

The landlady looked disapproving. 'Oh, yes. George told me that. Silly idea, I think, to keep your family's name. You didn't choose your father—you did choose your husband. It gets confusing, too. Two names on the mailbox and all that inconvenient stuff.' She shook her head. 'I never will understand you young women.'

Devon swallowed hard and nodded politely. I'll take him apart, she thought, her good humour forgotten.

Jon was standing at the kitchen sink, chopping onions. His tie was loose, his sleeves rolled up, his tweed jacket tossed over a chair. He looked up with a smile. 'I'm not trying to take your job, but I thought whatever else you put into your spaghetti sauce, it has to include onions.'

Devon slammed her books down on the table, flung her coat towards the closet, and kicked off her wet shoes.

'We're not having spaghetti?' he hazarded.

'I just talked to the landlady.'

'Well, don't let it upset your week. She's not the best conversationalist in the world, but she tries.'

'She called me Mrs Hardesty.'

He shrugged. 'Perfectly good name. My mother has used it for years. It isn't as if she called you something naughty, after all.'

'You told her we were married!'

He held up a hand to fend her off. 'I did nothing of the sort, Devon.'

'Well, she got the idea somewhere.'

'I hope that you didn't disillusion her. I'd hate to be evicted mid-semester.'

'Evicted?' Devon's eyes were wide.

'Yes. You know, thrown out, put on the street, kicked out. She and George frown on immorality among the tenants. She told me all about it last week at the laundromat.'

Devon absently got the minced beef out of the refrigerator and put it on to brown. 'They'd refuse to rent us this apartment if they knew we weren't married?'

'Are you a slow study or what? Of course they'd refuse. Society frowns on living arrangements like ours.'

'But we aren't sleeping together.'

'How well I know.' He poured the onions into a sauté pan, and stirred them as they started to sizzle. 'You wouldn't want to change that, would you?'

'Why bother with me? You have Margo.'

'Margo isn't the one who's flaunting herself around this apartment in everything from too-tight jeans to wrap-around bathrobes that somehow never seem to wrap quite far enough.'

'You sound angry, Jon.'

'No. Just terribly frustrated. I'm beginning to feel great sympathy for Matt—and he doesn't even have to see you first thing in the morning when you're still rubbing sleep out of your eyes. Do you know how sexy that is?'

He sounded serious, but of course that was impossible, Devon thought. She decided to ignore him. 'Are you browning those onions in my butter?' she asked suspiciously.

'Of course. It is, after all, your spaghetti sauce.' His look dared her to challenge his reasoning. 'You didn't answer my question. How about changing the house rules?'

Devon didn't bother to answer. There were more important things on her mind right now. 'You're avoiding the real question, Jon, which is—how did the landlady get the idea that we're married?'

'It may have been,' Jon said thoughtfully, 'when George asked about the name for the lease. You were still off looking at the bedrooms, I think. I gave him both names, and when he looked at me strangely, I said, "Devon insists on keeping her own name. You know how independent women are getting to be these days." He may have concluded from that . . .'

Devon started to do a slow burn.

He leaned over and kissed the tip of her nose. 'You're so cute when you're mad,' he said. 'But really, Dev—would you rather have lost the apartment? We could have looked for weeks and not found anything else this nice.'

'There's a flaw in that logic, Jon. *We* wouldn't have been looking—at least not together.'

'I'd have spotted you in Burton's classroom anyway. I've always had a weakness for blondes.'

'And brunettes,' Devon added sweetly. 'And redheads.'

He sounded hurt. 'Now is that kind?'

'Meeting in the classroom wouldn't have been the same, anyway.'

'That's true. I wouldn't be nearly as frustrated.'

'And the landlady wouldn't think we were married. Honestly, Jon, how could you do this to me?'

'I can name a dozen women who would be delighted to pretend to be Mrs Hardesty.' He shrugged. 'You just have a hang-up about marriage, that's all.'

'It would be no surprise if I did,' Devon agreed. 'It takes a fearful toll of a woman, you know. She does all the giving. I don't think I'll ever get married. I can take care of myself, and I'd just as soon not rely on a man. Or be responsible for him, either.'

'What did I tell you?' The telephone rang. 'Want to flip a coin to see who answers it?' Jon asked.

'By that time it will have stopped ringing. I assume that you've explained me to your mother?'

'I tried. She wasn't thrilled.'

'I can't imagine why,' Devon muttered and picked up the telephone.

It was Julie. 'I'm trying to fit my wedding gown,' she said, 'and Mother just can't get it pinned right to suit me. Can I bring it over tonight?'

'Sure. I don't have anything to do except papers to write and books to read. I'd much rather gossip and work on a wedding gown.'

Julie laughed. 'David wants to know if Jon will be there. If he is, he said he'd bring me.'

Devon cupped her hand over the mouthpiece and asked Jon, 'Are you staying home tonight? You've made a conquest in my family.'

'Julie? Too bad she's already engaged. I'll be here.'

Devon reported, 'Dr Hardesty says he will be at home. You might as well come for dinner—it's spaghetti.'

'That would bring David from Outer Mongolia,' Julie said. 'We'll see you in an hour or so.'

Devon put the phone down. 'Your conquest is not Julie. It's David.'

Jon shrugged. 'I'll have to work on that.'

Devon stirred the minced beef and added tomato sauce and spices. 'Are you serious?' she asked finally. 'Do you find Julie attractive?' Jon and Julie? She had a sudden picture of the two of them together—the single-minded dedication that each possessed in abundance would make them an unusual couple. And if Jon broke up David's engagement, she'd kill him, she thought fiercely.

'Of course I find Julie attractive. I am not blind.' He didn't look up from the garlic clove he was peeling. 'And before you stab me with that paring knife—it is not the sort of attraction that leads to romance.'

She stirred the sauce thoughtfully. 'Do you read my mind?' she asked finally.

'Occasionally. It isn't difficult. Stick to English, dear—leave poker and politics to the professionals. Your face is far too transparent.'

They worked in companionable silence for a few minutes. Then Jon asked, 'I assume that we're not going to tell David about Matt?'

'I'd rather not.'

Jon shrugged. 'It's really none of his business. And if you do anything of the sort again, I'll strangle you myself.'

'I've been thinking about it.' She was slicing French bread, with her back to Jon. 'And I've decided . . .'

Jon grunted. 'I can't wait to hear this one.'

'It was pretty much what you said. I did ask for it. I shouldn't have gone to his apartment.'

'It was a natural assumption on his part. On the other hand, he should have gotten your message a lot sooner than he did.'

'I was confused about what I wanted,' Devon admitted quietly.

'That makes sense. Virgins usually are.'

'Why do you act as if there's something wrong with me being a virgin?'

'You do like him, right?'

Devon nodded.

'If you weren't a virgin, you'd have slept with Matt last night, enjoyed it, and never had a second thought.'

She puzzled that one out for a minute. 'You think I should have gone to bed with him.' She felt a little disappointed. 'But you said . . .'

'Don't you ever listen? Matt would be a bad choice for a first lover. He's pretty selfish, and his technique could use a lot of work. That's obvious—if he'd known what he was doing last night he could have seduced you without a whimper. I wish I'd had his opportunity. Unfortunately for me, though, I am a gentleman.'

Devon laughed in spite of herself. 'So what do you suggest a poor virgin do, Jon?'

He shrugged. 'Stay away from the boys, for one. They have just enough experience to be dangerous, like Matt. Look at it this way, Devon. You don't come to college to learn from other students; that's why colleges have professors. If you want to know something, learn it from somebody who understands the subject. If you want to know about making love——'

'I know! I'll run an ad in the newspaper and ask for applications.'

He said modestly, 'You could go a lot farther and do a lot worse than me.'

'You're joking.'

He looked offended. 'Now who's being insulting?'

'I didn't mean it that way. I just . . .' Her face was hot with embarrassment.

'You just never considered that anyone over thirty could remember what love is all about, right? You haven't taken anything I've said seriously, have you?'

'Something like that,' Devon murmured.

'You really are a mere child. In the meantime, never take your shoes off when you're with a man. Then you can always run.'

Devon looked down at her feet and twisted her toes in the velvety-soft socks. She looked speculatively at Jon.

He saw her toes wriggle and said hastily, 'You're perfectly safe with me. I don't get turned on by toes. You understand that I make no promises if you keep running around in that leotard outfit of yours.'

'I am taking a dance class, Jon. I have to wear the uniform.'

'So move the stereo to your bedroom. Or take your chances down here.'

'I'll watch out,' she said demurely. 'And I'll let you know when I decide whether to take lessons from you.'

'I'll be here,' Jon assured her.

'Unless of course you're with Margo, or . . .'

'You can't expect me to hang about holding my teeth,' he argued. 'A man can only stand so much temptation, you know.'

Devon started to assemble the ingredients for a chocolate cake, which happened to be David's favourite. Why, suddenly, did the mention of Margo make her feel sick? She'd brought the woman's name up herself.

'Doc Driscoll said you'd help with my book,' Jon said. He sniffed the spaghetti sauce appreciatively.

'I said I'd look at it and see if I wanted to take it on,' Devon corrected. 'Why on earth are you writing a book, anyway?'

'Somebody famous once said that every human being has a book in him.'

Devon looked up. 'He added that inside the person was usually the best place to keep it, too. So why write it all down?'

'All the best people do it.' Jon's tone was patient, as if he was instructing a very slow kindergartner. 'It keeps the candidate's name in the public eye when he starts running for president. Or whatever.'

'Oh. Are you planning to end up in the White House?'

'I haven't looked that far ahead yet.'

'I don't believe it. You just aren't telling. What's the book about?'

'Read it and see.'

'You're actually writing a book? It isn't all a publicity stunt?'

'Have I ever lied to you?'

'Frequently.' She scraped the cake batter out into a pan and absent-mindedly licked the scraper. 'Okay, I'll read it. But I make no promises about helping with it.'

His eyes were dark and pleading. Devon was not impressed. 'I really need your help,' he said. 'I can talk all day, but writing things down is not my best skill.'

'Any research?' She put the cake in the oven.

'I do my own.'

'Good. It's the thing I fear most about grad school. Writing a thesis doesn't bother me, but I hate research.' She shook her head.

'Shall I set the table?'

'If you expect to eat.'

He straightened place mats and put out four plates. 'I thought you weren't going to stay in school.'

Devon sighed. 'I'll probably apply. Doc Driscoll will give me no peace till I do. And if I don't find a job, I suppose I can borrow the money to stay in school. At least I won't lack something to do.' She shrugged.

'You have chocolate cake batter on your nose,' he pointed out, and reached for the towel to wipe it off.

She looked up into his eyes. She'd never paid much attention to him before, she thought absently. Oh, she knew that his eyes could sparkle wickedly, but she'd never noticed the network of fine, crinkly laugh lines around them. Or the absurdly long, fine dark lashes. Or the way his mouth curved, as if he seldom saw anything that didn't amuse him.

'Studying me for a test, Miss Quinn?' he asked finally.

'Just wondering . . .' Her voice trailed off as she realised how embarrassing it would be if he knew what she was thinking. She coloured a little. She'd been wondering if he had meant what he said, about making love to her, or if he'd just been teasing.

He must have been teasing, she thought. Any man who was dating Margo Dickinson couldn't be seriously interested in Devon. That woman was beautiful, by anyone's standards. And nobody would dare call her a child.

Jon had moved nearer. 'What are you wondering about, Devon?'

'Do you really think I'm attractive, Jon?' Then she felt like a total fool for even saying the words.

He smiled. 'Oh, yes. Would you like me to show you?' He bent his head. He was so near that his breath stirred a lock of hair on her forehead.

Devon said uneasily, 'The spaghetti sauce . . .'

'I'm only going to kiss you, Devon. That's all. I promise.'

Only a kiss, she thought. She'd been kissed a thousand times. What harm could that do?

She was quickly disillusioned. Being kissed by Jon Hardesty did dreadful things to her pulse rate, and her breathing. His mouth was warm and gentle against hers; he was absolutely undemanding, yet her heart was pounding at the sensations aroused by his kiss. He hadn't even bothered to put his arms around her. Devon was free; he was not holding her or forcing her. But nothing could have made her pull back from that magical contact.

He raised his head, and Devon swayed a little, trying to regain her balance. 'Well?' Jon said, and raised a questioning eyebrow.

'I've obviously never been kissed by an expert before,' Devon said breathlessly.

'You could set off a few firecrackers yourself.' His voice was just a little unsteady. 'Anytime you'd like to practice, I'll be available. And whenever you decide to get rid of the virginity problem . . .'

'I won't,' Devon said sharply.

Jon shrugged and pulled his tie off. 'You have to sometime,' he pointed out. 'Unless you want to be a sour old maid English lit teacher. Just be cautious about who you choose, and I do hope it's me. In the meantime, I'll be taking a cold shower.'

Long after he had disappeared around the corner of the stairs, Devon stood in the centre of the kitchen, staring after him. 'What in heaven's name is the matter with you?' she asked herself finally. She should have told him to mind his own business. She should have slapped him. She should have done anything rather than submit to that kind of treatment . . .

But it had been a very nice kiss, she thought, and answered the knock at the back door without a second thought.

Margo Dickinson stood on the step, swathed in a long heavy coat that must have been mink. Diamonds gleamed in her earlobes. She looked stunned when she saw Devon, in her comfortable old jeans and yellow sweater, at the door.

'I'm looking for Jon Hardesty,' Margo said. 'Can you direct me to his apartment?'

Devon stood back from the door. 'You've found it. Come on in—I'll tell Jon you're here.' Then a spirit of mischief touched her heart. 'He's in the shower,' she added gently.

Margo looked as if her knees were about to give way. She crossed the threshold with caution.

'Sit down if you like,' Devon told her. She hadn't reached the foot of the stairs yet when a shout came from upstairs.

'What did that damn cat of yours do with all of my socks?' Jon bellowed.

Margo sat down, looking a little shocked.

'Check under the bed,' Devon recommended. 'And by the way, Margo is here to see you.'

There was an abrupt silence from upstairs. Devon tried to hide her smile. It served Jon right; after all, she'd warned him that there would be trouble over this arrangement.

'Actually,' she told Margo in a confiding tone, 'I'm a student of Jon's. Political science is such a fascinating subject, don't you think? We're having dinner with a couple of friends.'

Margo's face was like ice. 'If he has plans for the evening,' she said, and started to rise, pulling the coat tight around her as if it were armour.

'Oh, please don't go!' Devon was on her feet too. 'He'd be terribly disappointed if he missed you. Would you like a cup of coffee? It's already made.'

Margo would have refused, but Devon had a cup in front of her before she could get the words out. Devon brewed herself a cup of tea and tasted the spaghetti sauce, adjusting the spices.

'You seem to feel right at home,' Margo commented drily.

'I do love to cook,' Devon answered. She knew she was adding fuel to the fire; she tried to stop herself, but the words just continued to pour out in the chatty tone of a Southern belle. 'Jon's a marvellous cook, too, did you know? He makes wonderful breakfasts.'

The stairs creaked as Jon ran down them. 'Hi, Margo. Are you slumming?'

Devon made a ceremony out of picking up her tea cup. 'I'll leave you two alone,' she said cheerfully. 'Stir the sauce now and then, would you, Jon? And don't forget our guests will be here in half-an-hour.' Smiling, she retreated into the living room.

She could hear the rise and fall of Margo's voice, but she couldn't make out the words. Sighing, she opened her book. How she wished she could hear what Margo had to say!

She actually became absorbed in the chapter, and it wasn't until Jon was in the living room that she looked up. 'How did it go?' she asked with unfeigned interest. 'Did you get her calmed down?'

'I think I'll just murder you now,' he threatened. 'It will save me so much trouble in the long run. Devon, why in God's name did you tell her all that stuff?'

'All what stuff? You're the one who got yourself

into trouble. ''Where are my socks?'' she mimicked. 'For pity's sake, Jon . . .'

'I didn't know she was here, dammit.'

'I knew it would cause trouble.' Devon opened her book again.

'Only because you decided it should.' He leaned over her and she curled up tighter under her quilt.

'I didn't say anything that wasn't true,' she said firmly.

'No,' Jon drawled. 'You only said that you're my student, and if you think Margo believes that political science is all I'm teaching you, you have a long way to go.'

'It's true. I can't help it if she doesn't believe it.' Devon looked up into snapping brown eyes that were dangerously close. 'And you did volunteer to tutor me in other things. That wasn't my idea.'

'You, young lady, need to be taught a lesson,' Jon growled.

'I suppose you think you're the one to do it.'

'I seem to be the only one with enough nerve to try.'

She held up her chin defiantly. 'Go ahead—wring my neck. That's what you want to do.'

His hands closed gently around her throat.

'Violence isn't so very far under your surface either, is it, Dr Hardesty?' Devon taunted.

'Strangling you wasn't exactly what I had in mind,' he murmured. His hands slid to her shoulders and in one swift, inexorable motion he pulled her off the couch.

Devon's feet were tangled in the quilt and though she struggled it was an uneven battle. In moments she found herself sprawled on the carpet, still half-wrapped in the quilt, with Jon beside her.

'So what are you going to do—tickle me till I say I'm sorry?' she asked. There was a laugh in her voice.

'If you're going to play adult games, you'll have to accept adult consequences,' Jon told her. He moved abruptly, and Devon found herself pinned to the floor.

'Uncle,' she said. 'I quit. I'm sorry.'

'Too late,' he said softly.

She turned her face away, and his kiss landed in the vicinity of her right ear. It didn't bother Jon, though; he settled down to enjoy nibbling her earlobe and outlining the sensitive triangle on the side of her throat with the tip of his tongue. Shudders of violent pleasure rocketed through her body.

This has to stop, she thought, and began to protest. He silenced her with his mouth, his tongue darting and probing, awakening forces and feelings she only dimly recognised.

'Stop,' she moaned.

'Why? I'm having fun. So are you, by the way.'

They both heard the knock on the back door at the same instant. 'It's David and Julie,' Devon said. Her hands went to her hair, frantically smoothing the tumbled blonde locks.

'Damn,' he said huskily. 'This is just getting interesting. Do you suppose if we ignored them, they'd take the hint?'

'Nothing really happened,' Devon said softly, as if trying to reassure herself.

'If they'd been five minutes later, my dear, we wouldn't even have heard them knock. I think I'll tell David this is no way to win friends.'

'Don't you dare say that!'

He smiled. 'I thought you said nothing happened, Devon,' he said softly and kissed her again, hungrily this time, as if he might not get the chance again. Then, reluctantly, he pulled himself out of her arms and went off to answer the door.

Julie came in with a swirl of snowflakes, the plastic bag in her arms full of white satin and lace. 'Sorry to be late,' she said.

'We didn't mind the delay,' Jon said. His eyes were mischievously warm. Devon swallowed hard and stirred the spaghetti sauce with far more care than it required.

'David's car is acting up again. I brought your dress, too, Devon. It's all finished but the hem, so we can measure it tonight.'

Devon was delighted. 'I can't wait to see it.'

'I can't wait to eat,' David announced. 'Spaghetti first. Then you two can play with dresses.'

'Never have I seen a man with his priorities so mixed,' Julie told Devon.

'It's a deal—if you do the dishes,' Devon told her brother.

As soon as they had eaten, they left Jon and David demolishing chocolate cake and discussing the mayor's race. Jon said that he'd made his choice on who to support; Devon would have liked to listen to his reasons. But the lure of white satin drew her upstairs to her bedroom.

Julie pulled the dress over her head, cautious of pins that seemed to protrude everywhere. 'I'll never tackle this again,' she declared. 'Sewing a wedding dress is crazy.'

Devon laughed. 'You're never supposed to need another one.'

'Believe me, if this marriage doesn't last, next time it will be a justice of the peace and I'll wear whatever is already in my closet. And if I have a daughter, she's eloping.'

'You aren't going to make my gown?'

Julie stopped in mid-motion, arms above her head. 'Is that an announcement?'

Devon said quickly, 'Of course not. I just meant that whenever I find Mr Right, I'll need something to wear.'

Julie finished settling the long skirt and turned her back to Devon. 'The zipper doesn't seem to lie flat. And we need another half inch out of each shaping seam, don't you think?'

Devon started to pin.

'I thought you had already found him,' Julie said. 'Mr Right, I mean. How is Matt these days? And when are we going to meet him? Are you bringing him to the wedding?'

Devon was glad that Julie couldn't see her face, for she could not control the embarrassed blush that rose in her cheeks. 'I doubt I'll invite him to the wedding,' she said finally.

Julie looked as if she'd like to ask questions, but she didn't press the subject.

'Aunt Eleanor knows about Jon, by the way,' Julie confessed. 'David opened his big mouth.'

'I'm amazed she hasn't been over to rescue me.'

'Oh, she doesn't know you're living with him,' Julie said hastily.

'I'm not,' Devon said drily, through a mouthful of pins.

'Oh, you know what I mean. It turns out that she's one of his biggest fans. She's dying to meet him— thinks he'll be a wonderful governor.'

'Poor Aunt Eleanor. She's always been doomed to disappointment.' She put in the last pin. 'How's that?' she asked, smoothing a hand over the slick satin.

It was late when David and Julie left; Devon busied herself in the kitchen, avoiding Jon, who had stretched out comfortably in his recliner with the cat on his knee and his pipe in his hand.

But finally she forced herself to go into the living room. She couldn't live like this, she told herself, jumping a foot every time he walked by. He just had to stop it.

He looked up, questioning, when she planted herself in front of his chair, hands on her hips.

'I think it would be safer if we didn't repeat that— what happened earlier this evening,' she declared.

'Do you mean the kiss and the little wrestling match?' Jon drawled.

Devon nodded.

'Safe, my dear, is sometimes not the most fun.' He rose, dislodging Cyan, who protested loudly. Jon walked across to the window and looked out at the snowflakes starting to accumulate on the street. 'Devon, we've been thrown into a difficult situation here.'

'It may be difficult for you,' Devon remarked. 'I was doing just fine.'

'That's the key word—was. As long as we were pretending not to notice each other, we managed. But we can't pretend forever.' He turned from the window and put his hands in his pockets. 'I wasn't joking, Devon. This is terribly hard for me. Every time I see that silly leotard . . .'

'I'll only practice in my bedroom. Cross my heart.'

He smiled at the panic in her voice. 'But it isn't only clothes, Dev. It's the scent of your hair, and the way you laugh. And you aren't immune to me, either.'

She could hardly deny that. 'Jon——' Her voice was hesitant. 'What's happening to us?'

'I'm not sure. I know this is an unusual time in both our lives. Come next summer we'll both go on to other things. In the meantime we're marking time, waiting for the next change in our lives.'

'You aren't staying at the university?' she asked quietly.

'Probably not. I'll go back to Washington, perhaps. Who knows? And you'll be moving to wherever your first job is.'

'If I get a job.'

'You will. But this is a strange little interlude in our lives. While we're waiting for summer to come, why shouldn't we enjoy the next few months? Together.'

'Have an affair, you mean.'

'I never liked that way of putting it—but yes, that's what I mean.'

'I don't want to have an affair with you, Jon.' Her voice was a little shaky.

She was halfway up the stairs when he asked lazily from the foot, 'Don't you want to? Or are you scared to? Think about it carefully, Devon. The answer means a lot to me.'

CHAPTER SIX

'THAT'S the last of them,' Jon declared in relief as he set two bags of food on the kitchen table. 'It must look as if we're expecting to be snowbound for the winter.'

'It can happen.' Devon was unpacking another bag. She put eggs and cheese in the refrigerator. 'I can't always get a ride to the supermarket when I want to shop. Besides, I hate to go in those places.'

'The prices?'

'Not only that. I hate seeing all those suburban matrons looking as if they just got out of bed. Hair rollers and hubby's shirt and . . .' She shivered. 'I always want to walk up to one and ask her why she's wearing the hair rollers. Where on earth can she be going that is more public than where she is?'

'That's a point,' Jon conceded. He draped his coat over a chair and started to sort groceries.

'I will never be one of them, that's sure. The cute little station wagon with the wood-grain sides and the dog and the two kids . . .'

'You have something against kids?'

'Only when they're part of the package. I was actually looking forward to meeting your triplets. Such paragons have to be seen to be believed.'

Jon had the grace to look a little ashamed of himself.

'Who is Jason, anyway? Since he obviously isn't the middle triplet . . .'

'He's my mother's butler.'

'Of course. You've always been a member of the privileged class. How does it feel?'

'I could write a book. And speaking of books, when are you going to start on mine?'

'I have. I'm still wading through your manuscript.'

Jon looked mournful. 'Putting you to sleep, is it?'

83

'It's better than hot milk, that's sure.' Then Devon relented. 'No, it really isn't all that bad.' She finished emptying a bag and folded it neatly. 'Thanks for taking me to the supermarket, Jon.'

'I'm glad I can do something right. It doesn't make much sense for us to continue this business of your food and my food, anyway.'

She slanted a look up at him. 'Does that mean you're going to continue using my butter?'

He snapped his fingers. 'Darn. I forgot to buy margarine.'

'You didn't forget it, Jon.'

'No, I didn't,' he admitted. 'I just hoped that you wouldn't notice.' He took a package of meat out of the bag. 'I'll grill steaks tonight if you like.'

'Medium rare. Baked potato with sour cream, and just a little garlic in the salad.'

He smiled. 'Since you obviously don't like the idea of steaks, we can always have hamburger.' He reached over her head to put a box away. His sweater sleeve brushed against her hair, and Devon's whole body tightened.

'Still running, Devon?' he asked quietly. His hand trailed gently down over the golden-blonde hair, brushed out in a stream down her back. When she didn't respond, Jon sighed and turned back to the food lined up on the kitchen table. From then on he was careful to work on the opposite side of the kitchen from her.

Why did he have to ruin everything, Devon asked herself unhappily. They got along just fine until he touched her, and then all the fun was over.

That teasing wrestling match had been days ago, but it still had the power to make her uneasy whenever she thought about it. And she thought about it far oftener than she wanted to. Sometimes in the middle of the night she found herself wondering what would have happened if Julie and David had come by just a little later. And she was forced to admit that she had wanted, that night, to know what making love was really like.

It wasn't very comfortable to realise just how close she had come to finding out, when only the night before she had run from Matt . . .

'You didn't answer my question, Devon. You have to stop hiding from yourself sometime,' Jon said softly.

Devon tried to ignore him, but his words seemed to echo in her mind.

There was another long silence. Then Jon said, 'I did remember to tell you that tonight is my first open house—didn't I?'

Devon was aggravated; then she told herself firmly that it was, after all, Jon's apartment, too. Maybe no one would show up. She tried to pass it off lightly. 'Is that why you bought all of the snack food?'

'Of course. But if you've ever seen students, you know they prefer homemade stuff.'

'Is that a hint?'

'Nothing elaborate. Something like a chocolate cake would do.'

'Are you still cooking steaks?'

'Yes. If you'll bake the cake. The future mayor may drop in, too.'

Devon made a face. 'I'll spend the evening at the library, or something.'

'Why don't you stick around? You might enjoy the experience.'

'Why? I don't care who wins the election. It doesn't make any difference; all candidates are the same. They make promises, but they don't keep them.'

'What kind of a citizen are you, anyway? You can't cast a sensible vote if you don't know anything about the candidates.'

'I don't vote.'

Jon stopped in mid-motion, his hand resting on the edge of a shelf above his head. Then he turned slowly. 'You don't vote?'

'I've moved around so much that I've never bothered to register.'

'All the more reason you should stay around tonight.'

'I think I'll work on my research paper. Thanks just the same.'

'I'll give you extra credit in Modern Problems.'

'The university would frown on that.' Devon would have pursued the subject, but the telephone rang.

It was Julie. 'At last you're home,' she said. 'I've been trying to get you all morning. Will you have lunch with me? I'm tied up in the organic chemistry lab till one, but . . .'

Devon had a sudden mental picture of Julie handcuffed to a gigantic Bunsen burner, surrounded by animated test tubes and beakers, one of which was telling her. 'We have ways of making you talk.'

She giggled. 'Sure, Julie. Will Portable Pies do, or shall we go somewhere fancy?'

'That's fine. And Devon? We have a problem.' There was something very near despair in Julie's voice.

'You and David have had a fight, right? Is the wedding off?'

'Not yet, but it might be.' Julie hesitated, and then said in a rush, 'Oh, Devon, I am such a fool. I didn't know how he'd take it, and it was easier to tell Eleanor to go ahead . . . I never dreamed the man would actually come.'

'Hold it!' Devon commanded. 'What did Aunt Eleanor do? And what man are we talking about?'

'Your father. Eleanor asked me if she should invite him to the wedding, and I told her it was all right, but now he's coming and David is absolutely livid with me . . .'

Devon was dead silent. She knew exactly how David felt, she thought. They hadn't seen their father since David was ten and Devon eight, but she well remembered the confusion and the hurt she had felt when he abandoned them.

Julie was waiting for an answer. 'It's done, Julie, and we can't change that,' Devon said finally. 'I never dreamed that Aunt Eleanor knew where to find him.'

'That's what I thought,' Julie said miserably. 'She's always threatening things that she can't deliver, and I assumed this was just another of them. But when David found out, he said he isn't having the man at his wedding, and that if he comes there isn't going to be a wedding.'

'He's angry, honey. Anyway, I'm sure we can find a way out of it. I'll meet you at Portable Pies at one.'

Julie sniffed and agreed. Devon put the 'phone down thoughtfully.

Jon handed her a cup of coffee. 'You look as if you need this. See a ghost or something?'

'Something like that.' Devon told him what Julie had said.

'You haven't even heard from your father since you were eight years old?' Jon questioned.

Devon's temper flared. 'Not directly. And you needn't think that's so damned odd. It happens a lot more often than you'd realise.'

'I believe you, Devon.' Jon's voice was gentle.

Mollified, she went on, 'For years we didn't know if he was alive or dead. Then he wrote to Aunt Eleanor—it was after Mother died. David tore the letter up and sent it back to him—said he'd never have anything more to do with the man. He blamed Dad for Mother's death.'

'Why?'

'She was working two jobs, trying to support us and pay off the debts Dad had left behind. She was exhausted, and there ... there was an accident.' Devon's voice broke.

'Debts?' Jon handed her a tissue.

Devon blotted the tears that blurred her vision. 'He gambled,' she said finally, with difficulty, 'and he drank. He left because he was sure that when he got to California it would all be better—the land of milk and honey, you know.' Her voice was bitter.

'Does he live in California now?'

'I suppose so. It's been years since that letter came; he could be anywhere. I always thought that the letter was the end of it. David was pretty definite about never wanting to hear from him again.'

'Perhaps your father has changed, Devon.'

'You don't know him.' She stared out the window, her fingers clenching the damp tissue into a hard ball. 'Well, he isn't going to ruin David's wedding. He isn't wanted here, and I'll tell him that.'

There was a long silence.

'It may not be such a problem, anyway,' she mused. 'I can't imagine that he has the money to make the trip, and if he expects David or me to send it to him . . .' She laughed, a bitter note in her voice.

Jon got up, poured himself another cup of coffee, stirred it thoughtfully. Then he sat down again across from Devon and said, 'Why don't you let me see what I can find out?'

'What are you going to do? Check out every Skid Row mission in California till you find him? Ask him if he's willing to show up sober? Come on, Jon.'

'I do have some resources, Devon. When's the wedding?'

'The end of March.'

'We have six weeks, so you don't have to get upset today. Don't jump off a cliff till you know what's below, Dev.'

'Wonderful. Remember that line; you can use it in a speech someday.'

'What will it hurt to wait? You can still tell him to go to hell a month from now. That will be plenty of time.'

'What about David?'

'I'll talk to David, too. He'll pay more attention to me than he will to you.' He sipped his coffee. 'Just let me see what I can find out.'

Devon was silent. He was right about David, she thought; David respected Jon's opinion.

'If you're thinking about calling your Aunt Eleanor, I'll bet she won't tell you where he is,' Jon speculated. 'She's not dumb; she'll know why you suddenly want his 'phone number.'

'How do you think you'll find him, then?' Devon challenged.

'I still have friends in California. Some of them are known as "Senator" instead of "Mister".'

Devon hesitated. 'You'd cash in political favours to find my father?'

Jon nodded. 'Let me try, Devon. Once I find out what he's up to, you and David can call him up and tell him whatever you want. I'll even dial the 'phone. But at least wait till you know what you're talking about.' He hunted out a pencil and notepad. 'Here. Give me his name and anything you know.'

Reluctantly, Devon did. 'Aunt Eleanor is a fan of yours,' she said, tearing the top sheet off the pad.

Jon smiled. 'Good. Then I'll start with her.'

Doc Driscoll was on the 'phone when Devon stopped by his office, so she sat down on the low ledge of the window just outside his door and stared down across campus. It was a gloomy dark afternoon, bitter cold under a lead-grey sky.

Devon sighed. This kind of weather didn't help anyone's mood; she and Julie had both been so depressed at lunch that they had almost ordered a beer to cry into. The problem was already a difficult one, and unrelenting gloom outside didn't foster cheerful attitudes. 'And it's only the middle of February,' she told the world in general.

Doc came to the door. 'What are you doing, talking to yourself out here, Devon?' he asked, rubbing his hands together.

She stood up. 'Just a good case of midwinter blahs,

Doc. I thought you'd like to see this.' She handed him an envelope.

Doc unfolded the sheaf of papers and studied them. Then he looked at her over the top of his glasses and said, 'It's about time, Devon.' But his eyes were gleaming with pride. 'I'm glad you're applying. The graduate school will be better for having you in it.'

Devon shrugged. 'I doubt they'll see it like that, but if you want to continue deceiving yourself . . . I still have to pass my entrance exams, you know.'

'You will.'

'Such confidence!' Devon teased.

'How's Hardesty's book coming along?'

'I've been reading it; I really haven't started to work. It's not bad. He has a way of expressing himself that comes across surprisingly well on paper.'

Doc looked at her quizzically. 'Hardesty told me a few minutes ago that you'd said it was pathetic.'

'I never said that. I said it put me to sleep a time or two, which it has . . .'

'Have you ever heard the word "tact", Devon?'

'Jon said he wanted the truth.'

'Hmmm. So we've progressed to first names, have we?' Devon coloured in spite of herself.

'I warned you to watch out for him.'

'I am, Doc. Believe me.' She reached for the envelope containing her application forms.

Doc held them out of her reach. 'All signed and everything?'

'Of course.'

'Then I'll drop it into campus mail myself this afternoon. Just to be certain you don't change your mind.'

'I wouldn't. It took an awful lot of work to get that filled out.' But Devon didn't argue for possession of the envelope. 'I had better get to Modern Problems.'

She was almost late. Jon was already sitting on the edge of the desk, swinging a foot, as the redheaded girl in the front row asked a question.

Devon was amused to notice that the entire feminine half of the class had moved forward and was occupying the front three rows of the lecture hall. She took her customary seat at the back and opened her notebook.

Matt dropped into the seat beside her. 'Hi, Dev. Have you gotten over being mad yet?'

'I'm not angry, Matt. I should never have gone to your apartment.'

'Well, you might watch out in your own place, too. Or is it your roommate's guy who's been answering your 'phone?'

Devon pretended not to hear. She hadn't known that Matt had called. Had Matt not left a message—or had Jon not passed it on?

Matt sighed. 'Want to go to the jazz concert with me?'

'Sorry. I'm busy that night.'

'I didn't tell you what night it is,' Matt pointed out.

Devon looked up at him innocently. 'I happened to check the fine arts calendar yesterday.'

'All right, I can take a hint. But I'd still like to see you, even if you did lead me on and then back out.'

Devon gasped. 'Lead you on? What in heaven's name do you mean? All I did was come to your apartment to watch television.'

Matt shrugged. 'It was pretty clear to me.'

'You self-inflated, pompous . . .'

From the front of the room came an amused voice. 'Miss Quinn—Mr Lyon. If your private discussion can wait a little, it is time for class to start.'

The expression in Jon's eyes did not match the light tone of his voice, and Devon suspected that he had been watching her since Matt came into the room. She supposed she should have felt protected, but she was angry instead. What did Jon expect Matt to do, anyway—she raged to herself—drag her out of the lecture hall by her hair?

She settled herself with a little flounce and picked

up her pen. Jon's grin reached his eyes this time, and he turned to the redhead in the front row. 'Now, Miss Carson, what did you list as the nation's ten largest problems?' he asked.

In the next hour, she saw a side of Jon that she hadn't suspected, as he prodded students to share their reasoning. Within minutes a lively discussion split the class into factions to argue the merits of their case. And Jon perched on the corner of the desk, inserting a word here and there, never disagreeing with anyone, but keeping the argument going.

He's picking a fight, Devon thought with sudden insight. He's got them at each other's throats, and they don't even know what happened. Students who had yawned through Dr Burton's lectures were sitting on the edges of their chairs.

It was Jon who called the discussion to a halt. 'Our time is up,' he announced, over the continuing argument. 'You'll have a chance to continue on Thursday. Come prepared to back up your arguments with evidence. And begin to think about which problem on your list that you want to study in depth for your midterm project. You'll get full instructions next week.'

Students started groaning all over the lecture hall.

Devon stacked her books. Matt, who had remained silent throughout the class, as if observing Jon, said, 'I'll buy you coffee. Let's talk.'

Devon shook her head.

At the front of the room, Jon said, 'I'd like to see your lists, please. Drop them off at the door as you leave. Miss Quinn, since you are already at the back of the room, perhaps you would collect them.'

Disgusted, Devon slammed her books down on her chair and stationed herself at the door. 'Obviously, I'm going to sit in the front row from now on,' she muttered.

'What does Hardesty have against you?' Matt asked.

Devon ignored him and tried to make order out of

the loose pages thrust into her hands from all directions by students in a rush to leave.

'He doesn't usually pick on people like that,' Matt mused.

'Maybe he doesn't like having English majors taking his courses,' Devon snapped.

'On the contrary,' Jon said, coming up behind them unnoticed. 'You add a little class to the class—so to speak. I have another section of that manuscript for you, Devon. Can you stop by my office, or are you anxious to get home?' His expression dared her to refuse the request.

'I'll see you later, Matt,' she said.

Jon watched with a speculative gleam in his eyes as Matt left the room. 'So you have a date with him.'

It was a moment before Devon answered. 'What business is it of yours if I do?' she asked irritably.

He raised an eyebrow. 'It became my business the moment you called me to rescue you, Devon.'

Devon was past the point of being reasonable. 'I'll date whoever I choose, whenever I choose. You don't own me.'

'I never said I wanted to,' Jon pointed out gently. 'I'll never again be so happy to get rid of a student as when Burton comes back at midterm and takes you off my hands.'

'Why?' Devon bristled.

'Because you distract me so. I keep having all kinds of thoughts that are not appropriate for the classroom.'

'Such as what?' she asked suspiciously.

'Such as how much I'd like to kiss you. It's a good thing nobody asked for my list of the world's ten worst problems. You were number one this afternoon.'

'Should I be flattered?' Devon snapped, but he'd already left the room.

Devon retrieved her books and debated about ignoring his request and going straight home. But she still had his papers. Well, she decided, she'd walk in, drop them on his desk, and walk out—without a word.

A fellow student stopped her in the hall, so it took a few minutes to reach Jon's office. She hesitated outside the door when she heard voices.

'What's this Stella tells me?' The voice was deep and vibrant. 'She's upset about some floozy you're living with.'

Oh, God, Devon thought. Here it comes. She drew back behind the door.

'I thought I should come and check it out,' the voice continued. 'Is your mother overreacting again, or is it true?'

'That's not quite the way I'd have chosen to express it,' Jon said quietly.

'So it is true,' the man said shrewdly.

'I assume that it took more than my behaviour to bring you to town. I'm not a teenager any more, you know.'

'That's not the only reason I came, no. Not that your behaviour isn't plenty to get me out here, Jon. What in the devil are you thinking about? The opposition will have all kinds of fun discussing your morals in the next campaign, son.'

Son? Devon put her hand over her eyes. She'd heard enough about Seth Hardesty from Matt to know that he had a reputation for ruthlessness. She wanted to fade away down the hall, but the stack of student papers was still in her hand.

'I doubt it. They'll be too busy explaining their conduct in office to throw mud about my private affairs.'

'Jon, this is not just another affair. Your mother says you've set up housekeeping with this one.'

'Let me get this straight. It isn't really my sleeping with her that's bothering you, is it?' Jon said.

'Hell, no. Sleep with her as often as you want. Just be discreet, Jon. No promises. Don't let her get any ideas. You know how to play the game.'

'I certainly do. You taught the subject well, Dad.' Jon's tone was dry.

'And you know what your mother and I expect, too. Why don't you get married, Jon?'

'I've thought about it. I don't like the idea.'

Seth went on as if there had been no answer. 'That's the thing to do. Get yourself a hostess who knows the rules. Then you can have all the playmates you want on the side. But this swinging bachelor stuff has to stop.'

Devon had heard enough. Her anger was still keeping her warm when she reached the apartment. She slammed the door behind her, flung the papers on Jon's desk in the corner of the living room, and went upstairs to take a shower.

Half an hour later Jon tapped on her bedroom door. 'Why didn't you stop by my office?' he inquired politely. 'I was waiting for you.'

Devon took her time about answering. She unplugged her hair dryer and put it away, folded her wet towel with precision and hung it up to dry, tightened the belt of her terry robe, and yanked the door open. 'I did stop. You were absorbed in an important conversation, so I brought your precious papers home. They're on your desk.' She leaned against the door frame. 'Did you explain to your father that there's a difference between living together and splitting the rent on an apartment?'

Jon shrugged. 'I didn't bother. He wouldn't have understood.'

'Really?' Devon said tartly. 'It sounded to me as if you understood each other very well. I feel sorry for your mother, actually.'

'Don't. She's quite content, and they see each other now and then. Actually they get along better now than before the explosion.'

Devon shivered. 'That sounds awful. I didn't know they were divorced.'

Jon looked startled. 'They're not. I was twelve, I think, when she caught him in bed with the upstairs maid. They've been sort of separated ever since.'

'Why didn't she just divorce him?'

'Be sensible, Devon. She has what she wants—the house, the summer home, the condo, the limousine, the servants, the charge accounts. They both do as they like, and they talk to each other about once a month.'

'You sound very cold about the arrangement.'

Jon shrugged. 'I love them both. The way they choose to live is up to them; I don't take sides.'

'It's certainly not my idea of a successful marriage.'

'Your parents didn't do any better, Devon,' he pointed out. 'Till-death-us-do-part is a fairy tale, like unicorns and mermaids.'

'You aren't upset? Because your father disapproves of your living arrangements, I mean.'

'Why should I be? And actually, he doesn't disapprove. He just wants me to be discreet.'

'If it's all so important to your father, why didn't he go into public life?' Devon questioned.

'He was too busy making the money so I could.'

'Living through you must not be much fun for him.'

'Oh, he has his reward in mind,' Jon said lightly. 'He wants to be ambassador to France or something. I expect I'll get his bill on Inauguration Day. Now, I'm going to take a shower. Would you care to join me? There's plenty of soap for us both, and I'd be delighted to scrub your back.'

'No, thanks,' Devon said, her face reddening. Then, as Jon started to laugh, she wished that she had called his bluff.

But the only thing wrong with that, she decided as she started to get dressed, was that Jon probably wasn't bluffing.

CHAPTER SEVEN

THE noise level was unbelievable. The argument that had started during class that afternoon had burst out again, a hundred decibels louder, it seemed to Devon, in the living room.

She curled up in a chair in the corner and studied the scene. The room seemed to be carpeted with people, most of whom she had never seen before. Jon was even more popular than she had expected; she couldn't think of any other instructor who could fill a room merely by announcing to his students that they were welcome to drop by for coffee.

She did recognise a few, of course. Matt was sitting on the carpet across the room from her. She had avoided him, but she was aware that he was watching her.

Jon had assumed his favourite posture, stretched out in the recliner, pipe in hand. He was enjoying the argument, putting in a word here and there, but mostly just observing the discussion and the students themselves. Cyan was curled up on his chest. Now and then she stretched a paw up to pat his chin, as if reassuring herself that he was still there.

The redhead sitting on the arm of the couch next to Devon was observing Jon. She looked up once and blushed a bit under Devon's inquisitive gaze. 'You're taking Modern Problems, aren't you?' she asked. 'I haven't seen you around the department before.'

Devon nodded. 'I don't take any more history than necessary.'

'Isn't he a living doll?' the redhead asked, tipping her head towards Jon. 'But somehow I didn't expect him to be a cat lover.'

'I suppose his attractiveness is a matter of opinion,' Devon said coolly.

The redhead looked shocked. 'Well—if you don't like the subject, and you didn't come to look at Dr Hardesty—then why are you here?'

Devon considered telling her, and then thought better of it. 'What's your reason?' she asked quietly.

The redhead answered with cheerful candour. 'A little of both. He certainly isn't the usual professor, is he? Of course, not many of them are rolling in money. I wonder if it would be worth the effort to go after him.' She didn't bother to wait for an answer; she slid off the arm of the couch and inched towards Jon's chair.

He was relighting his pipe, concentrating on packing scented tobacco tightly into the bowl. He lit a match, two frown lines furrowing his forehead.

Devon put her elbow on the table next to her chair, propped her chin in her hand, and studied him. What did the redhead—and for that matter, all the rest of the girls who had moved to the front of the classroom today—see in Jon Hardesty? she wondered.

The redhead dropped to the floor at Jon's feet and sat there, Indian-style, staring up at him with what Devon thought looked like adoration. How perfectly sickening, she concluded. Then Jon looked down at the girl, and smiled, and Devon felt a cold chill clench tight around her heart.

You are jealous, she told herself in utter astonishment. You are suffering from a bad attack of the old-fashioned, green-eyed monster.

Devon had experienced pangs of jealousy before, but the times she had suffered the emotion had been brief and fleeting. Usually it had been her boyfriends who were jealous of her. This time she was in actual pain.

Jon finally got his pipe lighted to his satisfaction, and he looked up suddenly, catching her gaze over the crowd. He winked, that wicked sparkle flaring in his

IT'S A JACKPOT OF A GREAT OFFER!

- 4 exciting Harlequin novels—Free!
- an LCD digital quartz watch with leather strap—Free!
- a stylish ballpoint pen—Free!
- a surprise mystery bonus that will delight you

But wait...there's even more!

Special Extras–Free!

You'll also get our monthly newsletter, packed with news on your favorite writers, upcoming books, and more. Four times a year, you'll receive our members' magazine, *Romance Digest*. Best of all, you'll receive periodically our special-edition *Harlequin Bestsellers* to preview for ten days without charge.

Money-saving home delivery!

Join Harlequin Reader Service and enjoy the convenience of previewing new, hot-off-the-press books every month, delivered right to your home. Each book is yours for only $1.66—29¢ less per book than what you pay in stores! Great Savings plus total convenience add up to a winning combination for you!

YOUR NO-RISK GUARANTEE

- There's no obligation to buy—and the free books and gifts are yours to keep forever.
- You pay the lowest price possible and receive books before they are to appear in stores.
- You may end your subscription anytime—just write and let us know.

TAKE A CHANCE ON ROMANCE–THEN COMPLETE AND MAIL YOUR SCORECARD TO CLAIM YOUR 7 HEARTWARMING GIFTS.

PLAYER'S SCORECARD

MAIL TODAY

FREE BOOKS
Free Pen & Watch Set

Did you win a mystery gift?

> PLACE STICKER HERE

☐ YES! I hit the jackpot. I have affixed my 3 hearts. Please send me my 4 Harlequin Romance novels free, plus my free watch, free pen and free mystery gift. Then send me six books every month as they come off the press, and bill me at just $1.66 per book (29¢ less than retail), with no extra charges for shipping and handling. If I am not completely satisfied, I may return a shipment and cancel at any time. The 7 gifts remain mine to keep.

NAME

ADDRESS   APT.

CITY

PROV./STATE   POSTAL CODE/ZIP

Stylish LCD quartz watch–
just one of your 7 gifts!

You'll love the appearance and accuracy of your new LCD quartz digital watch. Genuine leather strap. Replaceable battery. Perfect for daytime...elegant enough for evening. Best of all, it's just one of 7 wonderful prizes you can win– FREE! See inside for exciting details.

eyes, and turned back to the argument raging around his chair.

Devon continued to stare across the room at him. You'd better be careful, she told herself, or you'll discover that you've fallen head over heels in love with Jon Hardesty.

Then common sense reasserted itself, and she laughed at the idea. It was impossible. Devon had fallen in love a hundred times; it was a delightful experience. By now she knew the stages well. First there was the instantaneous, breathless attraction, then the carefully-played-out sequence that led to a first date. By the third date, the initial attraction had usually waned, and she was ready to settle for friendship. Sometimes the man involved was agreeable, sometimes he wanted more. If he pursued her, she turned away, and looked around for another man to whom she was attracted with that same breathless abandon.

None of that had happened with Jon. You're suffering from indigestion, she told herself bluntly. Or an over-active imagination. Just because the man was always around didn't mean that she would fall for him; if anything it should protect her, because she knew his faults so well.

Oh, did she know his faults, she thought. She knew that he hated vegetables, and that his definition of washing dishes was to put them to soak. She knew that he never refolded a used towel, and that he would hit the roof if she moved a single item on his desk. Small as they seemed, any of those things could drive a woman crazy, if her married friends were telling the truth.

But, she reflected, she also knew his strengths. He could get along with anyone, she suspected. David, who could be abrasive, was Jon's slave. He was gentle, and caring. Who else, faced with the problem of her father, would have reacted as Jon had that morning, with concern and willingness to spend his own time and influence to set her mind at ease?

And he could not hide the gentleness in his nature. At the moment, he was absently stroking Cyan. The cat, her eyes half-closed, managed to look lazily ecstatic as that strong hand massaged her soft fur. No, he couldn't fool Cyan; the cat preferred him and would only come to sit in Devon's lap if Jon wasn't around.

As if feeling her gaze, Jon looked up, and his hand stilled on the cat's satiny coat. There was no laughter in his dark eyes now; they were serious, with a hint of a question in their depths.

Devon looked away, nervously studying the textured pattern in the carpet. Jon Hardesty is dangerous, she told herself.

Matt caught her eye across the crowded room. He was frowning, and he obviously had observed her careful scrutiny of Jon. Well, that was Matt's problem, she decided; she couldn't prevent him from jumping to conclusions. She shook off her mood and walked across to the small table loaded with snacks. Thoughtfully, she spread cheese on to a cracker and ate it.

The young man beside her was loading his plate as if he hadn't eaten in a week. He gestured to the chocolate cake in the centre of the table. 'Have you tried that?' he asked. 'It's wonderful.'

It should be, Devon thought. I've made that recipe so often I know it by heart. But she looked up with a smile and shook her head politely.

He drew a deep breath and a look of admiration crossed his face. Devon sighed a little, inwardly. Nice boy, she thought. He was good-looking and eager to please and probably very sweet. But the last thing she needed right now was another boy with a crush on her.

'Which classes are you taking with Dr Hardesty?' he asked, his eyes never leaving her face.

She told him, silently thankful for Dr Burton's appendicitis. If it wasn't for Modern Problems, what excuse would she have given for being at Jon's open house? 'And you?' she asked politely.

'The graduate seminars. I signed up for all of them.'

'You don't look old enough to be in grad school.'

He looked upset. 'I'm in law school, actually,' he said with dignity.

'I didn't mean to embarrass you.' Devon looked him over again; he still didn't seem older than eighteen.

He unbent and added, 'My father—he's an attorney, too—says I'll have to be grey-haired before anyone trusts me.'

Matt reached for a potato chip, and his arm encircled Devon's waist. She looked up in surprise and caught his level, warning look at the young law student. The young man saw it, too.

'Didn't mean to intrude,' he said hastily, and hurried across the room with his plate.

'That was awful,' Devon said, her voice low but taut. 'He was only talking to me. You don't own me, Matt.'

'I didn't do anything,' he protested, with a grin.

'Perhaps not, but you threatened to.'

'I don't know why I bother,' Matt said. There was a hard note in his voice now. 'You were almost drooling over Hardesty a minute ago. What's so darn special about that guy?'

'You should know. You used to think he was God's gift to the world.'

'To politics, yes.' He waved a hand towards the bookshelves. 'The man reads poetry, for heaven's sake.'

Devon froze. She'd never given a thought to her books, lining the shelves, their titles hardly typical of Jon. She doubted that he had given them a thought. If Matt went beyond titles and took one of those books off the shelf, and saw her name inside the cover . . .

'Why do all you girls get soggy over him?' Matt complained.

'Maybe it's because he knows we have minds as well

as bodies, Matt. Think about it,' Devon said, and returned to her chair.

Jon couldn't have heard the exchange, but he had interpreted the body language correctly, Devon thought, if the sparkle in his eyes was any indication. The man never missed a trick, she thought angrily.

Footsteps sounded on the front porch, and the student sitting nearest the door reached up to turn the knob. Devon recognised the man who came in first; his picture had certainly been in the news often enough. The man that Jon insisted would be the next mayor of the city didn't look much like a politician to her; he wasn't tall and commanding, as she had expected. In fact, she thought, the man behind him looked far more the part. He was older, grey-haired, well-tailored.

Then he spoke, and the first tones of that vibrant voice identified him. She'd heard that voice behind Jon's half-open office door this afternoon; Seth Hardesty was now in her living room.

Her mind was whirling with possibilities; she wanted to jump out of her chair and run—to her room, to the library, out into the cold—anywhere that Seth Hardesty wouldn't be able to see her. Even though common sense told her that he wouldn't know her from a gatepost, Devon was trembling with fear that he would look around the room, spot her instinctively, and then, in thundering tones, denounce her as Jon's mistress and throw her out.

Instead, he politely acknowledged Jon's introductions around the room, graciously accepted a cup of coffee, and chose a chair next to Devon's. She squirmed uncomfortably and caught Jon's amused smile as he took in her predicament.

Damn him, she thought viciously. He knew his father was coming, and he didn't tell me. I'll get even with him if it's the last thing I do.

The argument had concerned an issue of the campaign, and as soon as the candidate had made himself comfortable, several students clustered around him, soliciting his opinions. 'This is all off the record, you understand,' he told them confidingly. 'Jon asked me to come out and talk to you, just between friends.' Eager nods reassured him of their co-operation.

Seth Hardesty leaned back in his chair and drank his coffee quietly, watching his candidate. Then he lit a cigar, making a ritual of it, and looked around for a place to dispose of his spent match.

Devon handed him an ashtray. 'I didn't realise the mayor's race in this little city was important enough to bring you here, Mr Hardesty,' she said quietly.

He looked surprised. 'It's the first test of any size since the November elections,' he said. 'After that fiasco, the party has to start rebuilding somewhere.'

'Does the future mayor realise how lucky he is to have such a distinguished backer?'

He chewed on the end of the cigar and looked her over, and Devon regretted opening her mouth. Then he laughed. 'Are you just a little cynical about party politics, my dear? Of course he knows. If we get him in here for a couple of terms, he'll be a solid base of support for years.'

'No matter whether he's qualified to be mayor or not,' Devon said demurely.

Seth Hardesty looked a bit alarmed. 'You don't work for a newspaper, do you?'

'Oh, no. I'm just curious, that's all.' Jon had asked the same question, she thought. Suspicion of reporters seemed to be a family trait.

'At any rate, he's highly qualified. He knows the city, he knows the issues . . .' He tapped the cigar on the edge of the ashtray.

'At least, he knows what to say about the issues that the parties have agreed to bring up during the campaign,' Devon admitted. 'What about the others, the human issues? Nobody wants to talk about those.'

He looked genuinely puzzled, but before he could question her, a student interrupted. 'Mr Hardesty, why did you continue to support the last President when he obviously . . .'

Devon thought, That wasn't your most brilliant performance, Quinn. She joined a group at the snack table, determined to keep her distance from Seth Hardesty. She should know better than to cross swords with him in the first place.

Her smartest course, she decided, was to fade into the wallpaper for now and then to say her goodbyes and disappear with the first group to depart. It would at least get her out of the combat zone.

'What do you mean, human issues?' asked a deep voice at her elbow. Seth Hardesty reached for a wedge of chocolate cake.

'It's not important.' She didn't look at him.

'It certainly sounds important to you. How are we to look at issues if they aren't brought to our attention?'

'All right.' She folded her arms. 'First, education. Why aren't any of you big shots getting upset about the fact that kids coming into college can't read, they can't spell, they can't write a coherent paragraph? People are graduating from college and still can't fill out a simple job application.'

'Isn't that a problem for local school boards?' he asked mildly.

'If it was, it would be occurring only here and there. This is nationwide, and some leadership from the top certainly couldn't hurt.' She didn't give him a chance to respond. 'Then there's the question of women's rights. That's going to be a political issue, as soon as women discover that they have power. Women are earning less today in comparison to men than they were ten years ago. And the Congress votes down the Equal Rights Amendment—again.'

'The states voted it down the first time,' he protested mildly.

'Funny, isn't it?' Devon mused. 'When it's something the leaders of this country think is important, they threaten the states with consequences if they don't fall into line. This must not have been important.'

Seth Hardesty took a bite of his chocolate cake. 'I'm sure there are more issues troubling you, Miss.'

'There are. We spend hundreds of thousands of dollars in finding cures for cancer and heart disease . . .'

He raised an eyebrow. 'Those are human issues. Do you suggest we stop?'

'Of course not. But we're ignoring the disease that kills more Americans in a year than cancer and heart disease put together. The cost in lives, in medical costs, in family suffering, is higher than any other disease. And we not only don't treat it, we promote it.'

'I beg your pardon?'

'Alcohol abuse, Mr Hardesty. You wouldn't allow television networks to advertise the best brand of cocaine, would you—or heroin? But common ethyl alcohol is just as dangerous. Maybe even more so, because it's legal. And we picture drinking as the sophisticated thing to do.'

'Alcohol?' he asked faintly.

'Yes. If it was discovered today, it would be classed as a dangerous drug, available by prescription only.'

He laughed. 'Are you suggesting a return to Prohibition?'

'Of course not; it didn't work. But there are things the government could do—eliminate the advertising, for one possibility. They won't, of course. It's too dangerous, politically, to take a stand on things like that. It would upset half of the adult population.'

Seth Hardesty looked her over with respect. 'You're a lady of definite views,' he commented. 'Have you considered running for office?'

Jon laughed, and Devon, who hadn't known he was standing behind her, jumped a foot. 'Devon doesn't even vote,' he said. 'Why don't you pursue that for your midterm project? You seem extremely interested.'

She shrugged. 'What's the use?'

'Convince me you've found the solution, and I'll take it from there in the Senate.'

'You're almighty certain that you'll get there, aren't you?' She noticed, out of the corner of her eye, that Seth Hardesty had drifted away.

'Yes.'

'If you're so unbeatable, why did you lose the last election?'

'Because I didn't work hard enough. I learned my lesson. It won't happen again.'

Devon looked doubtful. 'Well, put that promise in writing and I might consider doing the project.'

'I'll even seal it with a kiss if you like,' he offered.

'Stop joking, Jon. I'm sorry about getting into an argument with your father, by the way.'

'Don't be. It doesn't happen to him nearly often enough. And who said I was joking about the kiss? You look very kissable at the moment.' His voice was low, but there was a note in it that disturbed her pulse rate.

Devon didn't bother to answer. 'I'm going to leave when the rest of them do, by the way. I hope I can get my coat without being conspicuous.'

His face darkened. 'Try it, and I'll embarrass you so thoroughly that you'll never live it down.'

Devon swallowed hard, but it was obvious that he meant it. 'You're crazy,' she said finally. 'You can't want me to stay around and meet your father.'

Jon just smiled and moved away through the crowded room.

The party died slowly, students trailing off in groups, some of them still arguing in loud tones that carried through the crisp air. It was a wonder that the neighbours hadn't complained, Devon thought as she filled a wastebasket with paper plates and cups.

The candidate had left an hour earlier, but her hopes for a peaceful end to the evening had flickered out when she realised that Seth Hardesty wasn't going to leave with him. It was obvious now that Seth would be the last remaining guest, and Devon had to fight off the urge to grab her coat from the hall closet and disappear out the nearest door. If she could just get over to Julie's house ...

She might avoid the consequences tonight, but Jon would have the last word. He seemed to specialise in that, she thought, irritated. Why he even wanted to introduce her to his father was more than she could understand. It was asking for trouble.

She decided that the rest of the clean-up was Jon's responsibility and stooped to pick up the cat, who was stropping herself against Devon's ankles. 'What's the matter, Cyan?' she asked, holding the warm little body close. 'Is Jon ignoring you?'

Cyan put her paws around Devon's neck and began to purr contentedly, directly into Devon's left ear.

'Do you mean to tell me that's actually Jon's cat?' Seth Hardesty asked.

Devon looked up in surprise, realising abruptly that they were alone in the living room. 'Who else would she belong to?' she asked, trying to sound surprised that he had asked.

'Who, indeed,' Seth said darkly. 'Would you like a ride home?'

'She looked up, startled. 'No, thanks, I don't need one.' Then she improvised, 'I walk everywhere.'

'That isn't safe, in this neighbourhood, is it?'

Devon shrugged. 'Safer than anywhere else in the city. I wouldn't care to walk around downtown at this hour.'

Seth Hardesty started to laugh. 'Why do I feel that our friend the future mayor would be wise to get you on his side?' he asked. 'Are you serious about all these issues you've been telling me about? If you are, the party is looking for some young women with stamina and ideas. You seem to have no shortage of either.'

'Me? Go into politics?' Devon shook her head firmly. 'With my views?'

The front door closed with a bang and Jon came back in, cheeks reddened from the wind.

'Perhaps you are a bit young yet,' Seth mused. 'But a little maturity and some practice in tact and diplomacy and you have promise. Don't you think so, Jon?'

'Oh, I think Devon has all kinds of promise,' Jon said silkily.

'Thanks,' Devon muttered, and wished that she had a vase handy so she could break it over his head.

'But definitely you'll have to practice diplomacy,' Jon added thoughtfully. 'That's the art of calling a person a nasty name in such a way that he thinks he's been complimented. If you want to learn the skill, Devon, here's the man to teach you.'

'I think I'll stick to being straightforward. If I call someone a name, I like for them to know it.'

Seth handed her a business card. 'Whenever you change your mind, call me. Now, why don't you let me take you home? I'm guaranteed to be a safe escort. Right, Jon?'

'That's a matter of opinion, and I've heard several,' Jon told him.

Devon said quickly, 'Thanks, Mr Hardesty, but I would really prefer . . .'

Jon interrupted. 'What Devon is trying to say, Dad, is that she doesn't need a ride home because she is already home.'

Seth Hardesty's eyes narrowed, and he turned to stare at her, inspecting her with a concentrated stare. Devon felt a deep, embarrassed blush that seemed to rise from her toes and spread over every inch of skin. She glanced at Jon; he was entertaining himself by watching the emotions that played over his father's face.

Seth started to laugh. 'All right, Jon,' he said finally. 'That was a trick worthy of me in my best days. I will go home and tell your mother that the young woman in question is not a floozy ...' He glanced at Devon, and seemed astonished that the description didn't upset her.

'You aren't mad?' she asked finally.

'Should I be?' he countered. 'Was all that just a sham to impress me?'

'That's the real girl, Dad,' Jon said lazily. 'Now you see what I have to put up with. It's no picnic to share an apartment with Devon. I have to be on my best behaviour all the time.'

'Don't press your luck, Jon,' his father warned. 'I'm only prepared to believe so much.'

'Then please believe this, Mr Hardesty,' Devon pleaded. 'We are not having an affair. We're simply dividing the cost of the rent. Honestly, that's all.'

He quirked an eyebrow. 'If that is true, young lady, then my son's judgment is even worse than I thought. I'll just go, Jon. I have an early flight in the morning— do you want to meet me for breakfast at the hotel?'

Jon agreed and walked his father out to the rental car parked on the street. When he came back, Devon was huddled in a chair.

'He didn't believe me, Jon,' she accused. 'Why did you do that, anyway? Why didn't you just let me go with the rest of the kids?'

'Because if I hadn't introduced you, he'd have thought I had something to hide. And if I'd told him straight off who you were, he'd have based his judgment on that. The way it happened, he got a jolt that will take him all week to figure out—he was very impressed with you, before he found out that you're the floozy he came out to see.'

'I'm shaking, and you think it was all some kind of joke.'

'Well, isn't it? We're both adults, Devon. What could he do, anyway, besides make a lot of noise?'

'He could disown you.'

'He wouldn't. I'm his only son, his pride and joy,

his—whatever other clichés you want to attach.
Besides, he can't cut me out of his will. My
grandfather took care of that. Aren't grandfathers
wonderful?'

'I wouldn't know. I never met mine.'

'I'm sorry. I'd forgotten.' Jon yawned. 'I'm going to
bed. Are you coming?'

'Just what does that mean?' Devon asked tartly.

Jon grinned. 'Whatever you want it to mean,
darling. After all, we now have my father's permis-
sion.'

She threw an ashtray at him; he ducked and it
bounced harmlessly off the wall. 'Does that mean you
have a headache?' he asked, and retreated up the stairs.

CHAPTER EIGHT

DEVON finished her coffee and refilled her cup. Time
for a break, she thought, pushing aside the technical
journal she had been reading. Cyan, who was watching
the birds gathered at the feeder just outside the
kitchen window, turned her head at the rustle of
paper, as if to tell Devon that she didn't appreciate the
interruption.

Devon stared out across the frozen street, absently
stroking the cat's chin, and then coloured as she
realised she was watching for a man in a brown
jogging suit to come up the sidewalk, ready for his
morning coffee. She'd been thinking that Jon had been
gone longer than usual, and wondering if he was all
right.

'Dammit, Cyan,' she said, 'I'm standing here
fussing about Jon like a teenager with a first
boyfriend. What's the matter with me, anyway?'

In the last two weeks, since Seth Hardesty had been
in town, they had settled back into a normal routine.
Jon jogged every morning, and Devon worried about
him being out in the bitter cold. He made an
occasional pass, and she fended him off, never quite
certain if he was teasing or not, never quite knowing if
she wanted to find out.

He hadn't seen Margo Dickinson in days, though,
Devon realised, and then was ashamed of herself at the
warm, contented feeling that swept over her.

'So what if he dates Margo?' she told Cyan crossly.
'Who cares?'

You care, came the answer from the back of her
mind. You care very much. Because you don't want
Jon to make love to Margo. You want him for
yourself.

Cheeks flushed with embarrassment, she tried to deny the truth that had jumped out at her. She couldn't do anything about it, she told herself crossly, and tried to imagine telling Jon that she had changed her mind. He'd laugh ... 'And then he'd be very sweet and considerate and take me to bed,' she said under her breath.

It would be only the beginning she knew that; the beginning of an affair that could have no happy ending. He'd said himself that it was an interlude in their lives, a brief span of waiting before they again took separate paths. Devon told herself firmly not to be a fool and sat down at the table, trying to renew her interest in research.

She was poring over a magazine article, frowning over the unfamiliar terminology, when Julie knocked at the back door. Her breath was frosty in the bitter air and she pulled off her gloves and rubbed her wind-reddened cheeks as soon as she was inside. 'I'm glad you're home,' she said. 'If I'd had to walk back across campus without a chance to warm up they'd have found me frozen into a heap next spring.'

'It must be something important to get you out of the lab at this hour of the morning,' Devon laughed.

Julie gratefully took the cup of coffee Devon offered and sat down at the kitchen table, doing a double-take when she saw the titles of the books stacked at her elbow. 'You're reading biochemistry?' she said. 'It's actually a new novel, right?'

'No, it's for real.'

Julie glanced down the stack of titles. 'Why have you been hiding out in the science library?' she asked.

'I'm doing research for my Modern Problems project.'

'Reading medical books?' Her tone implied that Devon had finally flipped.

'It's my paper on alcohol abuse. I told you about it, didn't I?'

'Oh. I forgot.'

'It's fascinating, really.' At least it is, she told herself, when I'm not thinking about Jon instead. 'Did you know that more than half of fatal traffic accidents involve at least one drinking driver?'

'Devon, the only thing I know about alcohol right now is that I'm scared to death your father will show up at my wedding smelling of it.'

'I'd almost forgotten.'

'Well, I haven't. And David hasn't either.'

'I thought Jon had talked to him.'

'He did, but that was two weeks ago. Now David's being very cool again, and he's doing crazy things like refusing to let the rental place take his measurements.'

'That sounds like David.'

'He says if that man shows up he won't need a tuxedo. I don't know if I should push him or leave him alone.'

'He is unpredictable,' Devon agreed.

'And the wedding is now less than a month away. I'm really in a jam, Devon. Does Jon know anything new?'

'I haven't asked him, but I don't think he's had a chance to look into it. He's had father problems of his own—his dad was in town for a while.'

'I can't picture Jon having a father.'

'Well, Jon doesn't take him too seriously. Of course, he never takes anything seriously. I did, and was laughed at for my pains.'

Julie stared into the bottom of her mug. 'Sometimes I long for the good old days,' she mused. 'Then there was nothing to worry about except my next biology test and whether I had a date for Saturday night.'

'I know. I even miss dormitory living sometimes— cafeteria food and all.'

Julie looked up with a smile. 'I'll never miss that.' She drained her coffee cup. 'If you find out anything, please let me know.'

'Have another cup, and you can ask Jon yourself. He's coming up the driveway.'

Julie turned to look out the window. 'I thought his car was parked out there.'

'It is. He's jogging.'

'In this weather?'

'He says it's the best kind.' Devon reached for another mug and filled it. Two minutes later when Jon burst in, breathing hard, she handed it to him.

He wrapped his hands around the mug and looked down at Devon, bright-eyed and contented. 'You are becoming very well-trained, my dear. Good morning, Julie.' He draped the top layer of sweatclothes over the back of a chair and stretched out in it. 'The streets are slick. It was more like skating than jogging, actually. What brings you here, Julie?'

'Have you found David's father?'

'Yes.'

There was a moment of strained silence. 'Is he actually coming to the wedding?'

'Yes.'

Devon burst out, 'You didn't tell me!'

'You didn't seem to want to know. Any other questions?'

'Well, he might as well not bother,' Julie said bitterly. 'If David finds out, there won't be a wedding.'

'Don't tell him.'

'Some help you are,' Devon snapped. 'You were going to tell Dad not to come.'

'Did I say that?' Jon asked politely. 'I thought I was simply going to investigate the circumstances.'

'What if we don't want him?' Devon blazed.

Jon said thoughtfully, 'Weddings are public functions, you know; you can't prevent his sitting in the back row of the church to see his son get married. He isn't asking to be invited to the reception.' He pushed his chair back. 'Anyone for a doughnut?' he asked, holding up a bakery bag.

Devon ignored him. 'And that's all he's going to do? Sit in the church and not even tell David he's there?'

'That's right.'

'I don't believe a word of it. How will he get here, anyway? Hitchhike?'

'Something like that.' Jon didn't sound interested.

'How are we supposed to keep it a secret?' Devon demanded.

Jon put a finger under her chin and gently pushed up. 'Like this,' he said. 'Whenever you get the urge to start talking, close your mouth.'

Julie pushed her chair back. 'Well, I hope you can explain it to David,' she said. Disappointment and concern dragged at her voice.

Suddenly serious, Jon put the doughnut down. 'I'll talk to him,' he promised. 'It will be all right, Julie.'

She shook her head. 'You don't know David as I do,' she warned. She pulled her gloves on, and tucked curly hair up under her knitted hat. 'I'll see you later, Devon.'

Devon watched her walk down the drive. 'You made a mess of it, Jon,' she said finally.

'I understand David's reasons. But I also see C.J.'s point of view. And right now I am caught in the middle.'

She turned to stare at him. 'You're calling him C.J.? We certainly got chummy quickly, didn't we?'

Jon ignored her. 'All he wants is to see his son get married. He'll come to town the day before the wedding, and leave the day after. It's a reasonable enough request.'

'Where does he live, anyway?'

'Los Angeles.'

Devon's eyes narrowed. 'He's coming halfway across the country for two days?'

'He might be willing to stay longer if you invited him.'

'Thanks, two days is plenty. What I meant was, he's coming all that way just for the wedding?'

Jon shrugged. 'It is his only son.'

'Dad always tried to do everything on a larger and more elaborate scale than anyone else would have.'

'On the other hand, perhaps that's all the time he can take off from his job.'

'You're joking. He has a job?'

Jon shrugged. 'He didn't exactly say that.'

'I'm not surprised. You're putting a lot of faith in the word of a man who has never been known to keep promises, you know.'

He didn't answer, and Devon thought he looked worried. And good enough for him, she thought. He ought to feel that way!

Devon's head was splitting. She stared at the piles of index cards, lined up in rows on the kitchen table, and thought for a moment that she was seeing double. No, she realised with a sigh, there really were hundreds of cards there. With an effort, she refocused her eyes and picked up another pile. At the rate she was going, it would be five years before she got all the bits of this puzzle assembled into a midterm project that would convince Jon that her ideas should become national policy.

Tonight, she thought grimly, she'd settle for a passing grade in Modern Problems. It was no satisfaction to realise that living with the professor would not guarantee her that.

And it certainly wasn't helping that the said professor was in the next room with a group of student volunteers at the moment, addressing and stuffing envelopes with campaign letters for the future mayor. In fact, Devon thought, if the noise continued, she might just pretend to be an irate neighbour and call the police.

'Do we have any more popcorn?' Jon asked from the doorway.

'There might be a bag in the lower cabinet.' Devon didn't look up. She rubbed a hand across the nape of her neck. 'Are you feeding the starving hordes of Africa in there, or what?'

Jon laid a hand on her shoulder, and Devon's spine

straightened. 'Sit still,' he ordered. 'I'm not going to
hurt you.' He started to massage the back of her neck,
his thumbs working up and down the taut muscles.
'Why don't you come in and join us?'

'Because I'm working. Or trying to, at least. Look,
Jon, next week is midterm, and I have to study. All
those fruitcakes in there may be willing to sacrifice
grades to elect a mayor, but I'm not. So would you
move election headquarters back downtown, please?'

Jon's hands hadn't paused in their soothing
massage. He had worked his way down to her shoulder
blades, and now he stooped to kiss her earlobe. 'I'll
get rid of them,' he promised, his voice husky. 'I love
it when you want to be alone with me.'

Devon twisted around in her chair. 'Dammit, Jon,
that's not ...' Then she saw his grin and knew that
she'd risen to the bait again. Irritated at her own
gullibility, she picked up her pencil, shaded her eyes
with her other hand, and concentrated fiercely on the
section she was writing.

'Did you know that Prohibition really wasn't a
failure?' she asked, trying to change the subject.

Jon was headfirst into a cabinet. 'Oh? If it worked
so well, why didn't they keep it?'

'In the years when drinking alcohol was illegal,
suicide rates dropped drastically, divorces were cut in
half, all kinds of illnesses became less common. People
drank less and were more careful because it was illegal,
so they got into less trouble.'

'Wonderful. With that kind of reasoning we should
make driving illegal, and then nobody would have
accidents. They'd still drive, of course, because they
have to get to work somehow, but they'd be more
careful.' The telephone rang at his elbow, and he
picked it up. A look of puzzled irritation passed across
his face. 'No,' he said, 'this is not Mr Quinn.' He
handed the receiver to Devon. 'It's for you, Carrie
Nation,' he said.

Devon held it away for a moment and said, 'If you

don't believe what I'm saying about Prohibition, just wait till you see the statistics.'

'Statistics can prove anything. Did you know, for instance, that a hundred per cent of people who eat dill pickles die?' Jon retorted and left the room.

'Of course they do, eventually!' she called after him, but Jon didn't answer. 'There goes your grade,' Devon told herself, and tried to be philosophical about it. It was just her luck to end up on the opposite side of the question from the professor. And it had to be a question that she felt strongly on. She couldn't even hedge her opinion.

She sighed and put the 'phone to her ear.

The caller was one of the few bright spots in Devon's practice teaching career. She remembered the girl with fondness; Sara shared her fascination with certain old poets. Most of Devon's students hadn't even recognised the names.

'Miss Quinn, I'm so excited! The university accepted me for next autumn's class.'

'Was there ever any doubt?' Devon laughed.

'I was afraid I wouldn't get in.'

Devon could remember the excitement; hers had come not when she was accepted, but when the university had confirmed that, because of her mother's long-time employment, her tuition would be free.

'I just had to let you know. If it hadn't been for your encouragement, I'd never have applied.'

'I'm glad you called, Sara.'

'And please tell your husband I'm sorry I called him Mr Quinn. I just didn't think, but of course he couldn't be, could he? I guess I didn't expect you to be married, because you didn't say anything about him last autumn.'

'Oh—didn't I?' Devon asked vaguely. 'How careless of me.'

By the time she was off the telephone, silence had fallen in the living room. Unable to believe her ears, she peeked in, and saw Jon straightening up the mess and talking in a low tone to Cyan, who was sitting atop the stereo and awarding him all the attention she felt the lecture deserved.

'And no more chasing your ball,' he told the cat. 'It makes too much noise when it bounces. We'll have to give up potato chips for the duration, too—they crunch. And if you could learn to walk quietly so the bell on your collar doesn't ring . . .'

Cyan stared at him with wide, unblinking eyes, and then jumped down from the stereo, walked straight to the metal wastebasket beside Jon's desk, pulled it over with a bang, and retrieved a crumpled cigarette pack that one of his students had discarded there. The cellophane rattled as she swatted it, chased it across the room, and lost it under the couch.

Devon started to giggle. 'Shows you what she thinks of you,' she told Jon as she picked up the cat. She snuggled her nose into the soft fur, and Cyan uttered a tiny meow of protest at being held.

'Wasn't it marvellous? We've been rehearsing that trick for weeks.'

'I do appreciate the quiet,' Devon said, suddenly serious. 'I have my grad school admission exams this week, too, and I don't want to be tired going in.'

'Absolute silence,' Jon promised. 'I'll even brush up on my sign language.'

He was almost as good as his word. For most of the next three days, he was gone. When he was present, an occasional rustle was all that she heard from him. It began to wear on her nerves, and by the evening of the third day she was ready to have it out.

She knocked on his bedroom door.

'Be quiet, there's a love,' he answered. 'Devon's studying.' Then he opened the door. 'You amaze me. I thought it was another of my women friends sneaking in to keep me company. Or have you changed your mind about having me as a lover?'

Devon ignored the remark. 'Why don't you stop trying for sainthood and just be ordinary?'

'You're hurting my feelings, Devon. Whatever else I am, I will never be ordinary.'

'That's true,' she mused. 'I'll try to be specific, Jon. Would you stop tiptoeing around the apartment, and hiding in your room, and going out to meals?'

'Ah. You're upset that I'm eating out.'

'No, I'm not. But I'm not going to assassinate you if you make a noise. I can't study here; it's too darn quiet.'

He looked wounded. 'I wish you'd make up your mind.'

'There is a happy medium between King Tut's tomb and the New York Stock Exchange. Munching your corn flakes is not going to make me flunk a test.'

He looked mildly interested. 'How about a basketball game?'

'Are you going to watch it on televison or bring the players here?'

'Neither. It's down at the auditorium, but I didn't want to interrupt you to tell you where I was going.'

'Go!' Devon almost yelled.

'That's just it. I hate to go to basketball games alone. Want to come along? You'll study better after a break.'

'You'll be lucky if it isn't you that I break,' Devon threatened.

'Then it would be silent all the time,' he pointed out. 'How did you ever manage when you lived alone?' He started down the stairs, and Devon trailed him helplessly.

It was something that she had begun to wonder lately. In previous semesters, she had isolated herself for the week before tests, laying in a supply of easily-prepared food and taking the 'phone off the hook. The only noise allowed was that of Cyan's purr as she lay on Devon's lap.

This year the silence bothered her. It's only because he's trying so hard to be quiet, she told herself.

Jon stopped at the kitchen door. 'Last game of the

season,' he told her. 'If they win this one they have a chance at the championship.'

'I have admissions tests tomorrow. No passing grade, no graduate school.'

'Cramming for those things is like studying for a blood test,' he scoffed. 'It's impossible. If you don't know it by now, you'll only confuse yourself by trying to study.'

'Some stand for a professor to take, Dr Hardesty.'

'In case you hadn't noticed, this professor doesn't believe in tests.'

'I'd rather take a test than write that awful paper for Modern Problems.'

'Cheer up, Devon. Burton will be back right after spring break.'

Devon groaned. 'He's even worse.'

'What an endorsement for me. May I have a written copy to attach to my resumé?' He pulled her coat out of the closet. 'Besides, you can raise your grade just by registering to vote. It's too late for the special election tomorrow, but you'll be all set for the future.'

'I can't believe you made that a class assignment, just because I don't vote.'

'It wasn't you,' he argued. 'I had just never thought about it until you came along. Do you know that only half of my students were on the rolls? Most of them have taken care of it.'

'Most of them aren't . . .' Devon broke off.

'Dumb enough to fight the system?' Jon said sweetly.

'It's a matter of principle, Jon, and I'm not registering.'

He shrugged. 'Suit yourself.'

'You're campaigning, anyway. You just want me to vote for you next time.'

'Is it so obvious? You really shouldn't complain about the results if you don't get involved in the system.'

'What if I vote for your opponent?'

'If that's what you plan to do, don't register. Come on. Let's shake the cobwebs out of your brain.'

'I don't want to go to the basketball game.' But it did sound like fun—the roar of the crowd, the excitement, the contrast to the quiet hours of study.

'You'll love it once you're there. I'll have you home by midnight—you'll get plenty of sleep before the tests.'

She slid her arms into the heavy coat. 'If I flunk them I'll sue you.'

Jon grinned. 'If you pass, can I choose my own kind of thank-you?'

The graduate admissions tests were awful. Devon was one of the last to leave the testing centre, and she had so little energy left that walking home looked like too much work. She went in the front door because it was closer and threw herself down in a chair, still wearing coat and gloves.

Jon put his pen down and turned from his desk to observe her. 'You look tired,' he said finally.

Devon didn't open her eyes. 'You get ten points for your powers of observation,' she said.

'It's one of my best qualities,' he said modestly. 'How did the tests go?'

'What a waste of time. I'll never get into grad school. I might as well have saved my trouble.'

'At least you tried.'

'Thanks for all your confidence,' Devon mocked. 'What are you doing?'

'Grading papers. It's no fun from this end, either.'

'I thought you had assistants to do that.'

'I prefer to do my own. It's my turn to cook tonight—would you prefer Mexican or Chinese?'

'Chinese. But we don't have a wok.'

'Amazingly enough, I know of a restaurant that does. My treat. Go change clothes.'

'I'm too tired,' Devon objected.

'All right,' he said. 'Be ungrateful. Stay home and

eat peanut butter. I'm sure someone will go with me.'

He'll probably call Margo, Devon thought glumly. 'You're a bully, Jon. Give me a hand, all right?'

'To get dressed?' he asked, eyes sparkling.

'No. Just help me get out of the chair.'

He pulled her to her feet, brushed her rumpled hair back off her forehead, and unbuttoned her coat. Then his hands slid to the small of her back and pulled her close against him.

Devon's heart was pounding. It had been weeks since he had kissed her, and she hadn't even known till this moment how much she wanted to be in his arms. She raised her head, lips parted, inviting his kiss, and let her hands trail sensuously over his shoulders and up to clasp at the back of his neck.

'Have you changed your mind, Dev?' he asked huskily. His lips brushed hers with fire, and his hands wandered up under her sweater.

'No,' she said, and choked on the word. She pulled away from him, horrified at her own behaviour.

His face was dark with anger. 'You're playing with fire, and you don't even recognise the flame,' he accused. 'You need to be taught a lesson.'

Devon stood there for a moment, frozen with shock. 'I'm sorry,' she murmured. 'I don't understand what's happening to me.'

It stopped him, but she could see in his face the struggle he was having for control.

Devon swallowed hard as she turned towards the stairs. She might just as well have ripped off his clothes, she thought angrily as she shut herself in her room. She couldn't have made it more obvious that she wanted him.

But as soon as he touched her—What is the matter with me? she asked herself angrily.

Devon tossed herself down across her bed, anger at herself churning in her stomach, along with frustration and absolute fury at Jon because he had provoked her response. She buried her face in her pillow, but she was too angry for the tears to come.

His footsteps sounded outside her door and she froze. What would she do if he came in?

He tapped at the door. 'Devon?'

'What?' Her voice was breathless.

'Don't panic, love,' he said. 'I came up to say I'm sorry, and to see if you're coming with me or staying home to pout.'

She didn't answer.

'It's all right, Devon. I'm quite aware that you scared yourself to death downstairs. I won't push you.'

So she'd scared herself, had she? But the anger was gone out of his voice. That was something to be grateful for. 'I'm coming. Give me two minutes to get dressed, all right?'

'Take five if you need it.'

'How generous of you!' she said tartly.

'I thought so. Our reservation isn't for an hour.' Whistling, he went on into his own room. Devon yanked clothes from her closet with unnecessary force.

The restaurant was not in a good neighbourhood. 'Where did you hear about this place?' Devon asked grimly as they walked past what looked like a flophouse.

'It looked all right in the Yellow Pages,' Jon shrugged. 'Where is your spirit of adventure?' But even he looked doubtful when he saw the garishly-painted paper lanterns. 'I hope the food is better than the atmosphere,' he commented under his breath as the waitress led them to a table.

'It could hardly be worse,' Devon said. 'Chop suey is probably as Oriental as this place gets.'

Jon opened his menu. 'Next time we'll go Italian. Nobody can mess up spaghetti, right? Someday I'll take you to a little Chinese place in Georgetown. It's so authentic you have to take an interpreter.'

Devon's throat was tight, but she tried to keep her voice light. 'Someday, when I happen to be touring

Washington, right?' She didn't look up from her menu.

She could feel his gaze and could imagine, because she had seen it so often, the quizzical light in his eyes. 'Right,' he said, and she could hear the smile in his voice. 'I'm sure someday they'll let you chaperon a school tour or something.'

'I'll call you at the White House.'

'You do that. By the way, we're stopping by election headquarters after dinner to join the celebration.'

Devon glanced at her watch. 'Jon, the polls don't close for another hour.'

He just shrugged. 'You have no faith, Devon.'

'I'll bet the other guy wins.'

Jon's eyes brightened. 'Shall I name the stakes?'

'Five dollars,' Devon said firmly.

'You are no fun at all,' he grumbled. 'I'm dangerous to bet against, you know.' His menu rustled. 'I'll be darned. Under the appetisers they list drunken chicken. I wonder what it tastes like.'

'Speaking of drunks . . .' Devon looked up demurely and sipped her tea from the tiny cup.

'Ah, yes. I talked to your father yesterday. He confirmed that he is indeed going to show up a week from Friday. He'll go back on Sunday, after the wedding.'

'That's three days. You said he'd only be staying two.'

'It was that or nothing.'

'Too bad I didn't have a choice,' Devon mused. 'Besides, that means an extra day of entertaining him.'

'He's a big boy. He can entertain himself.'

'I have no doubts about that,' she said tartly. 'But where is he going to stay?'

'What do you recommend?'

'How about Aunt Eleanor's extra bedroom? She's the one who invited him.'

'He said he wouldn't be comfortable there.'

'Well, he isn't sleeping on our couch. I won't have it.'

'He said he wouldn't like that either.'

'Oh?' Devon was suddenly irritated. 'What's wrong with him?'

Jon gave a shout of laughter. 'If that isn't just like you, Devon! You don't want C.J., but if he doesn't want you it makes you mad. He's staying at a hotel.'

'Well, that makes sense. Then he can drink if he likes with neither Aunt Eleanor nor I knowing about it. Not that I care,' she added, trying to keep a reasonable note in her voice, 'but how should he know that?'

'How indeed. I'm sure he'll feel more at home there anyway.' Jon closed his menu. 'What would you like, Devon?'

She gave her order to the waitress and waited for him. Then she asked, 'What do you mean—he'll be more at home in a hotel?'

'He lives in one all the time, in Los Angeles.'

'On Skid Row, right?' She tried to suppress her shudder. It was years since she had seen her father, but that didn't mean that she wished the worst for him.

Jon smiled. 'He didn't give me the street address.'

'You know what I mean, Jon.'

'I wouldn't call it a middle-class neighbourhood, no.'

The waitress set a bowl of what was supposed to be won ton soup in front of Devon. She stirred it suspiciously, and asked, 'Did you tell him about David? That he doesn't want him to come?'

Jon nodded. 'And that he's been threatening to call off the wedding, and all the nonsense. It's up to you to decide if David even knows C.J. is here.'

'Why me?'

'Because you're his sister, remember? After you meet your dad, you can either tell David or pass. C.J. will do whatever you want.'

'Why doesn't he just stay in California, then?' Devon said tartly. 'I could tell him that right now.

Why don't we call him tonight and settle the whole thing?'

'Can't.'

'Why not?'

'He's out of touch for a few days.'

'That means he's on a toot, right? And I'll bet he's been calling you collect, too. Jon, you are such a soft touch.' Shaking her head, she tried the soup, gave up, and pushed it aside.

'I know. I'm always trying to rescue damsels in distress.' He picked up her hand and snuggled it against his cheek. 'When am I going to get my reward? With everything you're putting me through, you'd better have a nice one in mind.'

CHAPTER NINE

IT was snowing, huge clumps of flakes drifting down to the white streets like so many miniature parachutes. The headlights reflected off the snow as the little green sports car made its careful way to the municipal airport. Devon, in the passenger seat, shifted nervously as the car skidded and then was firmly pulled back into line.

'I'll bet all the flights are cancelled,' she said.

Jon didn't look up from the street. 'It takes much more than a half-inch of snow to close a major airport, Devon.'

Devon was silent a moment. 'Why didn't you tell me he was flying?'

'You didn't ask.'

'Yes, I did. I asked how he was getting here, and you said he was hitchhiking.'

He shook his head, but she couldn't see his expression in the faint glow of streetlights as they flashed by. 'You assumed that. I just didn't correct you.'

'Where did he get the money?' She drummed her fingers against the leather upholstery. 'I bet you sent it to him, right?'

Jon grunted. 'Look, Devon, if you're going to have a nervous breakdown would you at least do it quietly? The streets are a little tricky.'

'I thought you said a half-inch of snow wasn't anything to worry about.'

'It isn't, on the runways. But they haven't cleaned the ice off the streets from last week's storm.'

'I wish you'd have told me he was flying.'

Jon shot a look at her in the dark car. 'Devon, I can understand if you don't want to call him Dad. I'm sure he won't mind if you call him C.J. But please refer to him as something besides "he" and "him" all weekend.'

'Thanks. I'll remember that it bothers you.' She dug her hands in her pockets and started to whistle tunelessly.

Jon muttered something under his breath.

Devon broke off and asked, 'What's the matter? Don't you like my whistling?'

'I've heard better.'

'You sound nervous,' she said, delighted to have found a crack in his composure.

'I am putting myself into the middle of a family feud here,' he admitted.

'Well, I think we should at least have told Julie he's coming after all. It's going to be a problem if he decides to go through the receiving line, and neither Julie nor David knows what's coming.'

Jon shrugged. 'They'll each think he's a friend of the other one. You know how those things go—you can walk along and smile and say "I murdered my mother this morning," and everyone will answer, "How nice!"'

'Maybe,' Devon said doubtfully. 'But it was not honest to tell Julie at the rehearsal tonight that you hadn't talked to Dad in two weeks.'

'It was the truth.'

'Perhaps it was the literal truth, but it wasn't honest. You knew she'd jump to the conclusion that he wasn't coming after all.'

'Think positive. Maybe he did back out.' Jon swung the little car into the parking lot.

Devon pushed open her door and gasped as the cold wind hit her full in the face. 'I couldn't have that kind of luck,' she called as she followed him across the lot and into the terminal building.

'Would you like a cup of coffee?' Jon asked. 'Glass of beer? Fifth of gin?'

'Are you telling me you'd like a drink while you wait?'

'I've had a few with less reason.'

'Coffee would be fine, thanks,' Devon said primly.

Jon sighed. 'I was afraid you'd say that.'

'I'll even buy, since I never paid off my election bet.'

'I tried to tell you never to bet against a seasoned politician.'

'That's why I never paid it. You took advantage of me.'

'Not as much as I'd have liked,' he said promptly. 'Next time I'll set the stakes, and then I'll insist on being paid.'

'You won't get another opportunity.'

'No more bets?' Jon sounded disappointed.

'I didn't say I wouldn't bet. But there are no more elections till next autumn.'

'What a shame,' he mused.

Once settled at a table, Devon started to stack the little containers of coffee creamer, building a tower six inches high.

'If you were three years old I'd spank you for that trick,' Jon warned. 'If you must be anxious, at least don't make a scene in the coffee shop.'

'What if the plane's not on time?'

'It wouldn't dare be late. Besides, this will keep you from being nervous about walking up the aisle tomorrow.'

She laughed a little at that. 'You're right; I'm far too worried about C.J. to let a little thing like falling over the hem of my dress bother me.'

'You'll be wonderful, even if you are far more upset than Julie is.'

'Why shouldn't I be? After all, Julie only has the wedding to worry about.' Devon wrapped her hands around her coffee mug and asked thoughtfully, 'Just what are you going to do if Dad turns out to be less than you expect?'

'Probably put him right back on the plane.'

'What if he won't go? I'm serious, Jon. You got him here; now are you going to see that he doesn't cause trouble?'

He lifted a hand in a Boy Scout salute. 'I faithfully promise to stick to C.J. like glue all weekend, in an attempt to modify damage to persons and property, till Sunday do us part.'

'What if he decides to stay longer?'

'You're strictly on your own after Sunday. I'm spending my spring break in Chicago, no matter what happens around here.'

She looked at him accusingly over the rim of the cup. 'You're going to leave us to cope.'

'Why worry? David and Julie will be gone on their honeymoon by then. Even if C.J. decides to stick around, all you have to do is lock the door and take the 'phone off the hook. What can he do, sit on the back porch and yodel?'

'I'm not convinced. Why do you have to go, anyway?'

He smiled, teeth flashing. 'Does that mean you're going to miss me, Devon?'

'Probably not,' she said with composure. 'Cyan might, though.'

'I'm glad we have that clear. I might have gone with false hopes if you hadn't set me straight. I, on the other hand, will miss you greatly.'

'Then why are you going?'

'In the hope that you will be so miserable without me that you'll be kinder when I come back. You don't understand the stress that it puts on a man when a woman treats him like a brother. You're driving me crazy, Devon.'

She wasn't sure how much of that to believe, but there wasn't even a sparkle of humour in his eyes. Devon wrinkled her nose critically. 'What are you going to do for a whole week?'

'Try not to mourn for you. It's been years since I've been to the museums, and I think I'll buy a whole new wardrobe to cheer myself up, and maybe call up a few old friends.'

Old female friends? The thought was instantly

followed by a stab of jealousy that Devon thought might split her in two. He probably would never be bored, she thought; there would always be a half-dozen women who would be delighted to entertain him. She stirred her coffee and wondered what his book would be like if he included all of the women. It wouldn't belong on the political science shelves, that was certain, she thought spitefully.

'You won't worry about me, will you, Devon?'

'Certainly not,' she said, a little more sharply than she intended. 'Anyway, I thought you were going to visit your mother.'

'I am. I haven't seen her since Christmas. She fondly believes that I have nothing better to do than spend a week dancing attendance on her.'

'Well, don't let it keep you from having fun,' Devon said sarcastically.

'Not a bit. I think they just called C.J.'s flight.' He pushed his half-full cup aside. 'You're starting to spoil me,' he added. 'I don't even like the smell of artificial cream any more.'

'Liquid chemicals,' Devon said loftily.

Her heart was starting to pound as they walked up the long ramp to the terminal gates. Would she even recognise her father? It had been nearly fifteen years since she had seen him, after all; she had been just a child. Come to that, would he recognise her?

She didn't even know that her hand was nestled in Jon's until he gave it a reassuring squeeze and looked down at her with that heartbreakingly attractive smile. How far she had come, she thought, from that first afternoon at Portable Pies when she had thought him a long way from handsome.

And that, she told herself firmly, is enough of that. It was far less dangerous to think of her father. She tried to pull her hand out of Jon's, but his grip tightened. 'Here they come,' he said, and Devon looked up the ramp with foreboding to the passengers coming towards her.

Just what did she remember of her father, she wondered. She had a vague recollection of curly blond hair, and a moustache, and vivid blue eyes. But was it her own memory, or what David or Aunt Eleanor had told her?

'I hope he doesn't try to kiss me hello,' she said in a voice that shook only a tiny bit.

Jon didn't answer, but his hand tightened on hers. It warmed her heart a little.

The plane had been full, and the stream of passengers down the ramp seemed never-ending. Devon took a deep breath and a firmer grip on Jon's hand and scanned the faces as they came towards her. This one was too young, that one certainly too old, another one surrounded by a family. There weren't many men alone, she thought, a little surprised. 'Aren't you going to hold a rose in your teeth, or something, so he'll recognise us?' she asked.

'He said he wouldn't have any trouble.'

'Dad always did have a high opinion of his own powers,' Devon muttered. 'Or will he be carrying a fifth of Scotch under his arm so you'll spot him?'

'Dev, why don't you just admit that you're scared to death?' Jon said quietly. 'Then you can stop all this blustering and everyone will be happier.'

'Especially you.'

'Do it to please me, then.'

Devon looked up with a challenge in her eyes. 'If you think I would go out of my way to please you, Jon Hardesty, then you are seriously mistaken.'

'We'll take that up at another time. I believe you have a visitor right now.'

Devon wheeled around to see a man coming towards them. His hair was white, his face lined, and he looked older than she had expected. But then he would be in his fifties now, Devon thought. His suit looked comfortable rather than fashionable, and it certainly wasn't new. But this was obviously no Skid Row bum. His skin was clear, his eyes bright, his step firm and steady.

C.J. stopped, just out of arm's reach, 'Hello, Devon,' he said quietly.

Her throat felt frozen. She swallowed hard and tried to say hello, but her voice came out in sort of a croak.

He smiled then, his face lighting up. 'This isn't easy, is it?' he asked confidingly, and turned to Jon, holding out a hand. 'You must be Jon.'

Jon let Devon's hand slip from his, leaving her feeling curiously alone. 'David couldn't come,' he said.

C.J.'s smile was rueful. 'Couldn't?' he asked softly. 'Or wouldn't?' He seemed to answer his own question. 'If he is still so adamant, perhaps it would have been better if I'd stayed on the West Coast, but . . .' He looked again at Devon. 'The flight has been worth it, just to see you again, Devon. You're not much like the little girl I abandoned, are you?'

The tears started to come then, and Devon wiped them away with the back of her hand, furious with herself.

Jon reached for her hand again. 'Let's pick up your luggage, C.J.,' he said. 'There's no sense in blocking traffic here.'

The snow was falling faster and was piling up on the streets. By the time her father was registered at the hotel, the streets were becoming dangerously slick. Devon was silent all the way back across town to the apartment, watching the hypnotic flicker of the wipers as they strained to keep the windshield clear.

It was nonsense to argue with the driver when street conditions were dangerous, she told herself. Besides, she hadn't decided what to say. She didn't know if she was angry at Jon for keeping the truth from her, or grateful that he had forced her to see her father again.

Once back in the apartment, Jon went straight to the refrigerator. 'I don't know about you, but I'm starving,' he announced. 'This business of meeting fathers causes great strain on my stomach.'

'Now you know how I felt when yours came to

town,' Devon snapped.

He rewarded her with a smile and started taking food out. 'Want a sandwich?'

'No, thanks.' She hadn't moved from the doorway or taken off her coat. 'You had dinner just a couple of hours ago,' she pointed out.

'I know. Thanks for reminding me; I must talk to David about his choice of menus.'

'At least the roast beef was hot,' Devon pointed out.

'Yes, but if he's going to remain a friend of mine he'll have to cut out the green beans.' Jon made a face and started to slice chicken.

'He hasn't had a drink in years,' she said.

'David?'

'You know who I mean.'

'Oh, you're talking about C.J. Yes, I heard him tell you.' Jon didn't sound interested; he was looking for the mayonnaise.

'He was sober when he wrote that letter to us, years ago—the one David tore up. You knew that all along, didn't you?' she accused.

'What if I did?'

'You could have told me.'

Jon looked up from the sandwich he had started to assemble. 'Would you have believed me if I had?'

Devon had to be honest. 'No.'

He shrugged. 'So I didn't bring it up.'

All of Devon's good intentions went up in smoke. 'You always think you know best, don't you? Haven't you interfered enough in our family affairs?'

'I'm finished, that's sure. I can't stand the strain. But I had the best of good intentions—I thought you might even be happy to see your father again.'

'It leaves me with a real problem! what do I tell David?'

'The truth might be a nice idea,' Jon mused. 'And speaking of truth, perhaps it's only fair to tell you the rest, too, Devon.'

'What do you mean?'

'C.J. not only lives in that hotel out in L.A.—he owns it. I thought you might like to know.' Whistling, he picked up his plate and left the room.

It had been a quiet morning. After the bombshell that had been dropped on her, Devon had decided that silence was her only possible defence; if she said anything to Jon she'd probably end up murdering him. And all the while his words echoed through her head.

I hate him for making such a fool of me, she thought. The very thought of all the self-righteous remarks she had made about her father left her feeling sick.

Jon had tried a time or two to start a conversation, but when he was ignored, he finally gave up. They drove to the church in silence, and it wasn't till the little sports car nosed up against the side of the red brick church where the wedding would take place that he tried again.

'Look, Devon,' he said. 'If you ever decide to come down out of the high boughs, I'd be glad to explain it all. In the meantime . . .'

'It must have been a lot of fun for you, wasn't it?' she snapped. 'Feeding me bits of information . . . Making a fool of me . . .'

'I didn't make you look foolish, Devon. You did that all by yourself.'

Angry tears sparkled in her eyes. She slammed the car door and plunged through ankle-deep snow to the steps. As she put a hand on the doorpull Jon said, 'Here's your dress. I don't think you want to escort Julie up the aisle wearing jeans.'

He draped the long plastic bag over her arm. 'Devon,' he said quietly, 'No matter what I said, you wouldn't have believed that your father was anything but a bum.'

She turned blindly away, knowing that he was right. It had been she who had jumped to conclusions, she who had made assumptions.

He opened the door for her. 'I'm going to pick up C.J. Any messages for him?'

She shook her head.

Jon hesitated for a moment as if there was something else he'd like to say. Then he brushed a gentle finger across her cheek and turned away.

She watched him with longing in her eyes as he walked back to the car. Why did it all have to be so complicated, she wondered. Why couldn't they just be friends?

David climbed the steps, blond head bare in the wind, hands in his pockets. 'Are you just going to stand here in the cold?' he said.

'Where's your car?'

He groaned. 'Don't remind me. The clunker gave out this morning—it looks as if it has really died this time.'

'David,' she said urgently, 'let's go somewhere for a few minutes. Just the two of us, and talk. It's the last time we'll have, before you're married and I'm . . .'

'Before you're what?' he asked, eyes intent.

'I don't know,' Devon admitted.

Julie came to the door. 'Come on in out of the cold,' she commanded. I can't believe the weather,' she complained. 'Only half of the wedding party is here yet. I thought you'd never come, Devon.'

'Julie, I need to talk to you and David.'

'Later, hon, all right? We have to start getting dressed now or we'll never make it. David, go get into that suit. It's going to take a while and the photographer will be here in a few minutes. Take your shoes off, Devon. The pastor's being a real bear about getting snow on his precious carpet.'

It was obviously no time to tell them about C.J. Devon stepped out of her snow-covered shoes and looked longingly at David, who shook his head and said quietly, 'It isn't the end of the world, Dev. We'll have that talk later, all right?'

*   *   *

The wedding went by in a blur. It might have been her own, she was so nervous, Devon thought in one of the few lucid moments of the afternoon. She mechanically marched up the aisle, stood and sat and knelt as she had been instructed. Julie's radiant face, framed in dark curls and white illusion, was one of the few things she remembered seeing.

The other was Jon. He and C.J. sat off to the side of the altar, out of sight of most of the congregation. But they were well within Devon's range of vision; when she took her seat to listen to the pastor's sermon she found herself staring directly at Jon.

His dark eyes met hers unflinchingly but without sympathy. Beside him her father sat, concentrating on the service. But Jon didn't seem to hear it; he was looking accusingly at Devon.

He doesn't understand, she thought despairingly, and then realised that it wasn't only C.J. that had caused the conflict. Why did there have to be such a wall between them?

Then she answered her own question. It's because Jon is powerful and well-known and wealthy and blindingly intelligent, and you are just Devon Quinn, a college student with a crush on him, she thought bitterly. No wonder he prefers politics to teaching; having all the co-eds falling in love with him must be boring.

In the reception hall pandemonium reigned as well-wishers clustered around the bride and groom. Julie's mother was trying to bring order to the mob when Aunt Eleanor cried, 'There's C.J.! He came after all, David!' and pushed her way through the crowd to catch up with him at the door.

In that instant, Devon saw it all—C.J. at the door shaking his head at Aunt Eleanor, and then being dragged back into the hall despite his protest; David turning to look down at Julie with something akin to disgust in his eyes; Julie's look of despairing unbelief as she stared at Devon.

Devon pushed through the crowd and seized David's arm. 'Julie didn't know he was coming,' she told him, her voice low and taut. 'You weren't supposed to know he was here, either of you.'

David turned on her. 'I said I didn't want him anywhere around, and I meant it.'

'David, he's a gentleman. If you tell him to get out, he'll go. But surely you can afford to be a good sport!'

He shook her hand off his arm.

A hush fell over the crowd as C.J. approached. Even Aunt Eleanor seemed to understand that she had caused a major problem, and fell silent.

'David,' C.J. said in that quiet voice, 'and Julie. I know that you're unhappy about me being here. I am sorry to have disrupted your day; believe me, I did not mean to do so.' He hesitated, then added softly, 'Best wishes to you both,' and turned away.

The crowd parted, allowing him to pass through easily. Devon was still, watching him, seeing in the set of his shoulders the deep unhappiness, the acceptance of David's right to reject him. And suddenly she couldn't bear it any longer. It wasn't fair for him to be alone like that.

She handed her basket of flowers unceremoniously to Aunt Eleanor, picked up the skirt of her long dress, and hurried across the room after C.J. She put a hand on his arm and said, with a smile despite the tears in her eyes, 'How would you like to take me out for coffee?'

His smile started deep in his brilliant blue eyes. He brushed a lock of hair back from her cheek and said, 'I'd love to, my dear, but this is your party too, and you belong here. It would be an honour, though, if you'd join me for dinner tonight.'

She nodded. 'I'd like that.' She looked up for an instant, and saw Jon's gaze fixed on her. There was a question in his eyes at first, but then he smiled, and

Devon's heart felt warm.

David was beside her a moment later. 'I didn't ask you to leave,' he pointed out to C.J.

'You needn't invite me to stay, either, unless you choose to,' his father answered.

Blue eyes met blue, and David's fell first. 'You've come a long way. You can stay if you want.'

There was a long moment of silence, then C.J. said, 'I'd like that, David.' He held out a hand. When David took it, Devon could almost feel a sigh of relief spread through the room.

It was a couple of hours later that Jon came up beside her at the punch bowl. 'I understand you have a dinner date,' he said. 'I've been invited to come along, if you don't mind.'

Mind? I'm delighted, she thought. But she merely said, with composure, 'I don't care. Come if you like.'

The sparkle in Jon's eyes told her that she wasn't fooling anyone. 'I'll give it some thought,' he drawled. 'I've so enjoyed meeting your Aunt Eleanor, by the way. She filled me in on all the details of your childhood.'

'She thinks it's so romantic that you're interested in me,' Devon said steadily.

'I gathered that,' Jon mused. 'It's a good thing that Aunt Eleanor doesn't know how you're treating me. It's cruel and unusual punishment.' He moved away through the crowd.

Devon set her glass down and slipped away to the little room where they had changed clothes. A few minutes of privacy would do her a great deal of good, she thought.

She was scared, and it had nothing to do with her father, she knew. The rush of joy that had flooded over her when Jon said he was coming to dinner was frightening.

'You have dinner with him every night, Devon,' she scolded herself. 'It's insane to be so pleased that he'll be there tonight.'

But there it was. Crazy or not, she was delighted.

It was a good thing, she decided, that Jon would be gone for the next ten days. She needed some time to think, to sort out just what she was feeling.

A knock on the door made her sit up straight. 'Devon?' said a girl's voice from the doorway. 'Julie's ready to throw her bouquet.'

'I'll be there in a minute.' She stared at herself in the mirror. I'm suffering from a schoolgirl crush, she told herself firmly. That's all it is, and I just need some time alone to get myself straightened out. By the time he gets back, I'll have myself under control.

She patted her hair into place and straightened her gloves, and hoped that the promise she had just made to herself was one she could keep.

CHAPTER TEN

THE week dragged for Devon. The campus was dead; most of the students had homes to go to. Even Portable Pies was closed so the owner could take his spring vacation.

By Thursday Devon was ready to climb the nearest wall. She had read till she had headaches, and watched television until she was suffering from terminal boredom. She had tried working on Jon's book, but his presence haunted the apartment as it was, and reading his work just made her loneliness worse.

Her father had called once. It had been soothing to talk to him, like finding an old friend who had been gone for years. But he was half a continent away, and as soon as the connection was broken, Devon's aloneness swept back over her.

She'd talked to Seth Hardesty, who called at the beginning of the week, trying to find Jon. When she had told him that Jon was visiting his mother, Seth had chuckled. 'That's the last place I'd expect to find that boy.' Then he had chatted for half-an-hour, questioning Devon about her research project and her views. She suspected darkly that Seth thought of her as a new public-opinion poll.

She had even tried to acquire a new skill and invested in yarn to knit a sweater. But the knots and snags and mysterious holes that appeared in her work soon left her disillusioned with that project too. It was almost a relief when Cyan discovered a half-finished sleeve and unravelled it all over the apartment, chasing it upstairs and down and knotting it around the furniture. It took Devon two hours to untangle the mess, which she dumped into the garbage can with a sigh of relief.

'That's the end of that dream,' she told herself firmly and went to the kitchen to bake a chocolate cake. At least it was something she could do well, and if eating an entire layer cake would make her feel better right now, she wasn't going to worry about the calories.

It would take something big to cheer her up, she knew. It was disconcerting to realise how much she missed Jon, how quickly his presence had come to be important to her. She had lived by herself for years, but how empty the apartment could seem now without him there, teasing her or playing with the cat or just working quietly at his desk.

'You've fallen in love with Jon Hardesty,' Devon told herself quietly as she stirred the cake batter.

It wasn't any kind of sudden, startling realisation; the knowledge had been growing in the back of her mind for weeks, it seemed to Devon. It was probably inevitable that she had tumbled into love with him; she had all kinds of experience with boys, but men of the world—sophisticated, knowing, experienced— didn't come into her life often. Jon was all of those things, and so it was no wonder that Devon had promptly fallen head over heels in love as soon as he had paid her a bit of attention.

'It's April Fool's Day, and you are one, that's for sure,' she told herself.

'And stop treating it like a terminal disease,' she added angrily. Devon had never believed that there could be only one important man in a girl's life; heaven knew she had been in and out of love so often that even she had trouble remembering just what stage she was in.

But this is different. Jon is different. The excuses sounded in the back of her mind, and she tried to argue them away. She certainly wasn't going to turn herself into a sour old maid if the first man she seriously wanted didn't want her. 'There will be other men, all kinds of them,' she told herself sternly. She tried to ignore the pain at the bottom of her heart when she thought of summer, in another apartment, probably in another town, with Jon far away.

But Devon was a survivor, and she would make it through this too. It would go away, this crazy crush on a man who thought of her as a child. It wasn't the end of the world.

'You'll be a better person for it,' she said aloud, and laughed as she realised how very pious she sounded. So she put the thought as far out of her mind as it would go and concentrated on baking the cake.

When Devon went out to get the mail, the landlady was beside the front porch, uncovering the flower beds. The air held a breath of spring, so Devon stood there for a few moments to talk. 'Isn't it early to be planting flowers?' she asked.

'Sure would be, but I'm not planting. I'm just taking the mulch off the tulips and crocuses. They'll be wanting to push up out of that dirt in the next week or so.'

'It doesn't seem possible that warm weather is so close.' Slow it down, her heart pleaded. Make it stay winter forever.

'Another week or two and you won't believe there was ever snow. That's the nice thing about the weather here; there's plenty of variety.'

'If you don't like it, wait a minute and it will change,' Devon agreed. 'I'm baking a cake, by the way. I'll bring some over for you and George.'

'What about that handsome husband of yours? As much as he brags about your chocolate cake, I don't imagine he'd appreciate you giving it away.'

Devon had long ago stilled her conscience; if the landlady wanted to believe that they were married, it wasn't really lying to let her remain contented and ignorant. 'He won't be home for a few days yet.'

The hand-rake didn't pause, but the landlady shook her head sadly. 'You young couples—I don't know what you're coming to. George and I have been married forty years and never spent a night apart. It's no good for a marriage when you aren't even in the same town.'

Devon idly flipped through the envelopes that she had taken out of the mailbox. Mostly for Jon, as usual, she thought. There was a stack of mail piling up for him on the corner of his desk. Then she looked closer at a buff-coloured envelope addressed to her. It was thin, no more than a single page letter. And it came from the dean of the graduate school. Was it acceptance, she wondered, or rejection?

She made a quick apology to the landlady, who muttered something about the ways of the younger generation, and went back inside. She dropped the stack on Jon's desk and walked on through the apartment, hardly knowing where she was. She stared at the envelope, afraid to open it. She wasn't even certain of what she wanted it to say.

Normally, with a letter containing such important news, Devon would have ripped it open. Instead, she hunted for a kitchen knife and slit it carefully, rinsed the knife and put it away, slid the folded stationery out of the envelope as cautiously as if it had been hot.

The doorbell rang, and she put the letter down on the counter and went to answer it.

Margo Dickinson stood on the step. Her mink had been left at home; today she was wearing a simple wool coat that had probably cost as much as Devon's whole wardrobe.

'Jon isn't here,' Devon told her.

'I know he's in Chicago. I talked to him last night. It's you I want to see.'

Devon stood back from the door silently, wondering what on earth Margo had to say to her. It would probably be less than pleasant, though, judging from the determined expression on Margo's face.

'Would you like coffee?' she asked.

Margo shook her head. 'No. What I came to say

won't take long.' She pulled out a chair and sat down at the kitchen table, her hands folded elegantly in her lap. 'I'm going to marry Jon,' she said flatly.

Devon was glad that her back was turned. She steadied her hand with an effort and finished filling her mug. By the time she came to the table, she had regained her composure. 'My congratulations. When is the happy day?'

'We haven't set one yet. Before his Senate campaign starts in earnest, of course. Probably before we go back to Washington this summer.'

'That's wise. It wouldn't be much fun honeymooning on the campaign trail, I'm sure.'

'Don't be naïve, Devon. Jon's more interested in a power alliance than a marriage, and my father can be a great deal of help to him. He's already offered Jon a job.'

'Sounds a bit disillusioning for you,' Devon mused.

Margo's eyes flashed. 'Don't waste a moment feeling sorry for me,' she snapped. 'I don't love Jon any more than he loves me. I haven't any desire to be in love.'

Devon sipped her coffee and made a face; she'd been so shocked by Margo's announcement that she'd forgotten the sugar. 'If you don't love him, why marry him?'

'Just how innocent can you be? I'm going to be somebody in Washington—the important people will beg for invitations to my parties. Jon has the money, and he will have the power, with Daddy's help, to do that. And he's the only man around who can make me First Lady someday.'

Devon took her time at stirring her coffee, staring at it so she didn't have to look at Margo. If she did, she thought, she might just throw the cup at that lovely cold face. 'Why are you telling me all this?' she asked, her voice deceptively calm.

'Because you're so damned innocent. Every girl he looks at thinks she's special, and when Jon moves on, she gets hurt.'

'Does this happen often?' Devon asked quietly.

'Every semester he teaches, there is one—a girl that he chooses and nurtures and pays special attention to.'

'And sleeps with?'

Margo's smile was cold. 'Of course. You're the first one he's moved in with, though.'

'Maybe I really am different, Margo.'

'Believe me, you're nothing special.' The tone was flat.

'So you're concerned that I'm having an affair with Jon.' Devon began to methodically shred the envelope that her letter had come in. 'Are you afraid that he might change his mind about you?'

'I'm not in the least concerned. It will pass—by summer you'll be only a memory. And don't flatter yourself, because he doesn't waste much time on memories.'

'You sound very calm about Jon's affairs.'

Margo shrugged. 'There will always be women. Jon's not the kind to be faithful to one, even if he was quixotic enough to think he loved her.'

Devon sipped her coffee in silence, trying not to show her shock. Had Jon ever seen this side of Margo? Had they discussed what their life together would be like? Then she remembered what he had told her of his parents' marriage, and she almost shuddered.

'As long as the women know how to play the game,' Margo said coolly, 'I don't care how many of them there are. But it's girls like you who don't know when the love affair is over. They're the troublemakers.'

Devon remembered hearing Seth advise his son to marry a woman who knew the rules of the game. Had Jon decided that his father was right after all?

'You still haven't told me why you're here, Margo.'

Margo stood up. 'Because sometimes when they get hurt, the girls try to get even, and then Jon has to be cruel. But I see you're like all the rest of them—too enchanted with his charm to wonder just what it is he sees in a little fool like you. You really think he's serious, don't you? That because he sleeps with you he means to marry you?' She pulled her coat close around her and stopped at the back door. 'Well, I tried to tell you. If you don't listen, then you'll just have to hurt worse when it's over.'

'I think that's my choice, isn't it, Margo?'

'Just don't fool yourself into thinking you can beat me. You can't, because I won't be beaten.' Margo flung the last words back over her shoulder as she walked towards her car.

Devon didn't bother to answer; she just closed the door gently behind Margo and wished that she had given in to instinct and thrown the coffee at her. Not that she believed most of what Margo had said, for she didn't. She didn't believe for an instant that Jon would marry Margo simply because her father was a powerful Senator . . .

Or would he? Bob Dickinson was a force to be reckoned with, and Jon wanted to go back to Washington. He didn't intend to be away from the centre of power for long. Was marrying Margo the price Bob Dickinson demanded for his support? And was that the reason that Jon was so certain that his future lay in politics?

'Jon isn't like that,' she said aloud, but her voice was small and breathless. 'Politics is a dirty business, but not Jon . . .'

And why not? her cynical other self inquired. Why should Jon be different from every other politician? The whole foundation of politics was compromise—the art of giving up one thing to gain another that was more important. No one, no matter how talented, could do any good unless he had power. She had seen Jon in action on election night, had seen the respect he commanded, had shared the magic. She had learned to respect his views over the months and to know that he would fight for what he believed.

Just how far would Jon go to get the necessary power and position to make his views known? To him, raised by parents whose own marriage was a sham, the very idea of marriage was a joke. Of course he would give up his bachelorhood to get the job he coveted. He would probably give up much more than that, if it was necessary.

Devon felt just a little sick. He could at least have told her himself, she thought. Or perhaps he had intended to, breaking the news to her gently, and Margo had decided not to leave it to him. After all, if Margo was right about the game Jon was playing, he would be in no hurry to tell Devon anything.

How could she ever have thought that Margo was beautiful? The woman was like ice.

Determined not to think about it any more, she took the over-baked cake from the oven and then picked up her letter from the graduate school. Whichever answer it was, she decided, at least she could begin to make firm plans. There would be no more hanging about, waiting for the decision to be made for her. And no more waiting to see what Jon was going to do. Devon was strictly on her own now.

'And I'm glad,' she told Cyan firmly. The cat stropped herself against Devon's ankles and then leaped up to the kitchen counter, begging to be held. She curled herself around Devon's neck and started to purr into her ear. 'You miss him, too, don't you?' Devon asked quietly. Cyan even searched the apartment for Jon, her unhappy meow seeming to echo in the empty rooms.

The letter was brief, just a few paragraphs saying that the graduate school was delighted to welcome her as a student. Devon stared at the letter for a few seconds in utter surprise. Then she did a quick waltz step around the kitchen with a startled Cyan in her arms. 'I'm in!' she cried. 'I actually made it!'

But the exhilaration was short-lived; within minutes she had come back to earth. It was quite delightful to be able to continue her education, but what was she to use to live on? Her plan for so long had included a paycheque starting in the fall; now she didn't know what to do. And now she would have tuition to pay as well as living expenses, since her free tuition would end with graduation.

Well, she'd manage somehow. She didn't dare turn down an opportunity like this. Doc Driscoll was right; there was always a way, if she wanted it badly enough.

She was asleep on the couch with Cyan draped over her feet, bored by television and the latest best-seller, when a noise outside roused her.

Just a branch rattling against the house, she thought indistinctly and settled down again. If there was nothing else worth doing this week, she might as well catch up on her rest. The apartment was dim; she had closed the drapes when she lay down on the couch, and dusk had come and deepened into dark while she slept.

But the noise sounded again, and then the back door creaked and footsteps tapped across the kitchen floor. Devon sat up straight, frightened. Had she locked the back door? Did she have a burglar inside the apartment with her?

She struggled out of the quilt which had been wrapped around her, panic slowing her movements. By the time she had freed herself and gotten to her feet, the footsteps had reached the doorway.

Then the light flashed on, and she stood blinking in the sudden brightness and looking at Jon across the room.

'You came home early,' she said, and smiled slowly. 'I thought I had a prowler.' Her heart was singing. He's back, she thought, he came home to me . . .'

'And I thought you were the prowler. All the lights were off; I was sure you had gone out.'

They stood there for a moment as if they were frozen. He was wearing a new jacket, a nubby tweed that her fingers itched to touch. He looked wonderful.

Devon put a hand to her tousled hair and said. 'I must be a mess . . .'

Jon shook his head slowly. 'You don't even know how beautiful you are,' he said softly.

She never did know which one of them moved first, but suddenly they were in the centre of the room, their bodies straining together as if they could not be close enough.

'My God, how much I've missed you,' he said, his voice rough. His hands cupped her face, caressing the supple skin, and then slid through the long glossy strands of blonde hair before he caught her close to him again.

All hesitation forgotten, Devon raised her face to his. That first kiss weeks ago had been unforgettable, but this one was even more powerful—wrenching every ounce of self-possession away from her and demanding that every inhibition be forgotten.

She tried to pull him even closer, wanting desperately to feel the ultimate closeness, to possess him body and soul, to share with him what she had never wished to share with any other man.

She let her fingers trail over the fine lines at the corner of his eye, down his cheek, across the firm, square jaw, and around his neck under the open collar of his shirt, till her hands clasped there to hold him tightly.

Jon smiled down at her. 'What a nice welcome home,' he murmured and lifted her off her feet to place her gently on the quilt she had dropped on the carpet. He was beside her there in an instant, his jacket discarded, her sweater disposed of with a quick pull. He cradled her in one arm as his other hand toyed with the buttons on her blouse, and his kisses feathered down on her throat, her cheek, her lips, till she was too breathless to move or even to think. All she was capable of was feeling, and Jon's lightest touch was setting her on fire.

'I'm glad you missed me,' he murmured in her ear. 'I thought perhaps if I went away, you would.'

Devon's muscles tensed. Ignore it, she told herself.

It doesn't mean he planned this. Just forget that he said anything . . .

'You've found a beautiful new way to celebrate, my dear.' He had reached the last button and spread the blouse open to bare her breasts, in the lacy bra, to his attention.

'Celebrate what?' she asked breathlessly.

He shrugged. 'Anything you like. Being together, my new job, warmer weather—take your choice.' His fingers were gentle as he toyed with her, drawing love lines on the delicate skin, tracing a path from throat to navel.

'Your new job?' A dreadful echo sounded as Margo's words that afternoon came back to her. Her father had offered Jon a job, she'd said . . .

'I really don't think this is the time, Devon. A little later, perhaps . . .'

'What new job?'

Jon sighed and stopped nibbling her earlobe. 'You have a one-track mind, don't you? I'm going back to Washington in June to run a special investigation for Bob Dickinson. Do you want to see the paperwork now or can we make love first?'

So his friend Bob Dickinson had come through. And Margo had known it this afternoon. But of course she had, Devon thought. Margo had talked to him last night. 'Don't touch me,' she warned.

'What do you mean, don't touch you?' His voice was puzzled.

'I mean, take your hands off me.' She tried to sit up, pulling her blouse around her. 'You planned this, didn't you? This little seduction scene?'

He wouldn't let her go. 'I didn't walk in here expecting this, if that's what you mean. If you hadn't thrown yourself into my arms, I'd have said hello and gone upstairs to unpack. From my point of view, it looks as if you heartily approved.'

'That was before.'

'Before what, dammit? What did I do?' He gave her

a little shake. 'It's a bit late to play innocent. You asked for this.'

Her voice was tiny and tense. 'I changed my mind, Jon. That makes it rape, you know.'

'I see.' His voice was dry. 'I feel a certain amount of sympathy for Matt Lyon. However, since I'm not quite as desperate as he was ...' He stood over her as she lay sprawled on the quilt and rebuttoned his shirt. 'It's your choice, Devon. I thought you'd made it, but apparently you still want to play games. When you change your mind about wanting to sleep with me——'

'You arrogant, conceited son of a——'

He cut firmly across her protest as if there had been no interruption. 'You'd better be convincing.'

She lay there on the quilt, cursing herself for the fool she was, trying not to shed the hot tears that blurred her vision and listened as he carried his luggage up the stairs. She jumped as he dropped the suitcases on the floor of his bedroom, right above her head, and wearily got to her feet, tucking her blouse into the waistband of her jeans, throwing her sweater over her shoulder.

So much for your dreams, Devon, she told herself. Margo was right. You did believe that under it all, you were different. You thought he really did care about you. What a fool you are.

It was five weeks till the end of the semester. Suddenly it was something to be endured, not savoured.

CHAPTER ELEVEN

IT was a relief when classes started again. At least Devon had something to occupy her mind with. Not that they had been cooped up in the apartment together; Jon hadn't spent more than twenty minutes a day there since he'd come back from Chicago. She didn't know where he was spending his nights. 'Probably with Margo,' she thought drearily.

What was really making her angry, she reflected, was the treacherous thought that kept popping up in the back of her mind. If she just hadn't asked questions, she would have been happy now. Jon would be coming home; this icy tension wouldn't exist, they would be back on those old teasing, fun-loving terms, with a new intimacy added. Certainly she would have been hurt later when he married Margo and took her back to Washington. But she'd have had some memories, too—some closeness to remember, some loving times to treasure. As it was, she had all the frustration and hurt and agony, and none of the precious moments.

And that just goes to show how messed up your thinking is, Devon Quinn, she told herself angrily as she came out of a classroom remembering none of what the professor had said. You don't care how much pain there would be next summer, if you could have a little fragile pleasure now. It was certainly not logical thinking, but it was exactly what was going on in her mind.

She was so preoccupied that she didn't hear Doc Driscoll call her name till he came to the door of his office and shouted down the hall after her.

Then she turned, startled, and said, 'Did you want to see me?'

'No, I just bellow students' names up and down the

halls for entertainment. Get in here.' But his smile was gentle.

Devon sat down beside his desk and twisted her feet around the rungs of her chair.

'Why haven't you been in to see me?'

'What about?'

'The grad school notified me that you've been admitted. Don't you want to apply for a teaching assistanceship?'

Devon shrugged. 'I suppose so.'

His eyes narrowed. 'Then I think we should get busy. Or are you backing out on me already?'

'No. I'll be here.' Her voice was lifeless.

'Devon, what in the hell has happened to you in the last few weeks?'

She looked him straight in the eye. 'Nothing of any importance, Doc.'

He stared back at her for a few minutes. 'I doubt that, but no matter. I'll call the dean and see what we can work out. You'll be teaching freshman English, of course.'

'There are worse fates in life.'

He chewed thoughtfully on the end of his pencil stub. 'What are you going to do if there isn't a position available?'

Devon shrugged again. 'Look for a job. I can't afford to stay in school without it.'

'You could borrow the money. Extend your student loans.'

'I don't have any, and I'd like to keep it that way. I've always worked to support myself, and my tuition was free.'

'What?' Dr Driscoll sounded stunned.

'You knew that, Doc. My mother worked at the university for years, so David and I got free tuition. But it won't pay for grad school.'

Doc shook his head. 'I don't know how you managed it, but this university doesn't give anyone a free ride.'

'I didn't manage anything. They recruited me and told me it was a benefit Mom had earned. And I don't care how it works, just as long as they don't send me a bill after I graduate.'

'You have me intrigued.' He reached for the telephone.

'Doc, for heaven's sake don't ruin it for me,' Devon begged.

'I won't.' A moment later he said, 'Hello, Annie. Do me a favour, would you, look up a student of mine in the computer. Devon Quinn. She's been on a full-ride scholarship . . .'

'Me?' Devon said. 'Scholarship? That's a laugh.'

Doc motioned to her to be quiet and continued, 'I just want to know if that will cover grad school tuition too. Thanks, Annie.' He cupped a hand over the 'phone and said, 'It made a good excuse to check the records, Devon. If you promise to be quiet, I'll let you listen in. But no more smart remarks, okay?'

'I promise. Sorry, Doc.'

He held the phone out and the two of them listened intently to silence on the other end of the line. Then a woman's voice came back on. 'Doc, you're wrong. There's no scholarship.'

'I told you,' Devon mouthed.

The voice continued, 'Her tuition's been paid in full at the start of every semester. We just mail the bills to her father, and he sends a cheque.'

Doc said, 'Thanks, Annie. I owe you one.' He put the 'phone down and leaned back in his chair, tenting his fingers together and studying Devon over the half-glasses.

Devon's face had gone white. 'Oh, my God, I wonder if the insurance is a lie too.'

'What does that mean?'

It was difficult to talk. 'Mom had a small insurance policy. They told us—David and me—that it would give us an income till we were through school. It isn't much, but it does keep the wolf away. Only now I wonder if there was a policy at all, or if that was Dad too.'

'You don't think he'd help you now?'

Devon shook her head violently. 'I won't ask him. I have a tremendous debt to pay to him already.' She stood up. 'Doc, I'll come back later. I need to think right now.'

She almost fled down the hall and collided with Matt at the lecture hall doorway. He caught her and set her back on her feet. 'What's the hurry, Devon? There's fifteen minutes till Burton will be here for Modern Problems.'

'I'm surprised you're early.'

'I just dropped my books off. I'm going up to Dr Hardesty's office to get my midterm project back. Do you have yours?'

Devon shook her head.

'Then come with me. I just hope I got a decent grade.'

Devon found herself propelled down the hall beside him. She started to protest, and then realised that if she was to avoid an argument with Jon, having another student along was the best way. And she did have to pick up that paper, someday. It might as well be now.

Not that there would be an argument, she thought wearily. They didn't argue these days. Mostly, in the little time they spent in the same room, they were icily silent. She was just thankful that her Modern Problems grade had been turned in before the spring break. If he was grading that paper now, Devon was afraid to think what the result would be.

Jon's door was locked. 'Damn!' Matt said. 'He's supposed to be having office hours now.'

Devon supposed that it didn't much matter to Jon. Another six weeks and he'd be leaving the academic community; probably forever this time. Why should he kick his heels around his office waiting for students to drop by and chat?

'He's been a real bear all week,' Matt mused.

Devon wondered if that meant that he wasn't sleeping with Margo, either. She wouldn't put it past Margo; after all, the woman had said that she had little interest in Jon as a man. And she's crazy, too, Devon thought. How could any woman not want Jon to love her?

'We might as well go wait for Burton to show up.' Matt smiled down at her, then. 'Hey, I'm glad you're over the little spat we had. Want to be friends again?'

It hadn't been Matt's fault, she thought. She had done the same thing to Jon. Maybe you're frigid, Devon, she told herself. 'Sure, Matt.'

'How about a movie tonight? There's one showing that sounds good.'

'As long as it isn't a gang war or something from outer space.'

Matt laughed and took her arm as they started down the steps. 'It's neither. It's a good old-fashioned comedy about a ghost. Somehow I doubt you're the horror-film type.'

'I'm not.'

As they reached the landing, Devon's whole body tensed up as she saw Jon coming up the steps towards them, two at a time. 'Dr Hardesty!' Matt said. 'We were just looking for you. Can we pick up our midterm projects?'

Jon was looking pointedly at Devon, accusation in his eyes. He hadn't missed a detail, especially Matt's possessive hand on her arm. Devon tipped her chin up and stared back at him with challenge in her eyes. After all, it was none of his business if she chose to walk down a hall with Matt.

It was the first time she'd actually been inside Jon's office, though she would never forget hovering in the hall that day while she eavesdropped on his conversation with his father. She looked around with interest, hoping to spot the kind of personal items that were so rare around the apartment. But she was disappointed. Jon apparently travelled light professionally, as well as personally.

He handed Matt's paper across the desk to him, thoughtfully flipped through Devon's, and looked up with a raised eyebrow. 'I'd like to discuss this with you, Miss Quinn,' he said. 'Do you have a few minutes?'

'I have a class.'

'What about afterwards?'

'May I at least see the paper now?' she countered. His hand lay atop it on the desk, and his index finger tapped gently on the cover page.

'You don't want to talk about it, do you?'

'I want to go to class, Dr Hardesty.' She pulled the paper out from under his hand and walked out of the office.

Matt followed. 'I see you and the great doctor have a personality problem,' he commented.

'You might say.'

'At least my grade was above average. Not bad, considering that I was expecting to have Burton's ancient multiple-choice tests instead. What did you get?'

Devon didn't answer. She was walking with her head down, paging through the paper. Notes were everywhere in the margins; Jon must have gone through an entire ball-point pen on her project, she thought bitterly. It went without saying, she supposed. Then she reached the last page and stopped dead in the centre of the hall.

Matt turned around to stare at her. 'Devon, we're going to be late. What's the matter?'

'He gave me an A.'

'That's hardly cause for a long face. Let me see.'

She wheeled around in the hall. She would get to the bottom of this, and she was going to do it immediately. Just what had Jon wanted to talk to her about?

'Where are you going? Hey, do you still want to see the movie tonight?'

'Yes. Call me later, Matt.' She marched straight back to Jon's office. She didn't pause at the door and she didn't knock. She simply walked in and stood over his desk.

'What's this, another bribe?' she demanded. 'Did you think that if I got the grade, I'd be so grateful I'd fall into bed with you?'

Jon raised an eyebrow and reached for the pipe that lay in the ashtray at his elbow. He leaned back in his chair and began to dig ashes out of the pipe with his office key. 'Whenever you've finished, let me know,' he said calmly. 'I hate to interrupt when you're having so much fun.'

'Well, you're absolutely wrong, Dr Hardesty,' she said, with elaborate emphasis on his title. 'I can't be bought. Just what did you want to say to me a little while ago? Were you going to explain how it happened that your judgment failed you so badly?'

Jon didn't even look at her as she raved; he merely cleaned the pipe, packed it with fresh tobacco, and lit it.

'Must you smoke that thing all the time?' she asked angrily.

'Why shouldn't I? It's my only vice.'

She laughed scornfully, but he didn't seem to hear. When the pipe was drawing to his satisfaction, he looked up and asked quietly, 'Have you finished?'

Devon nodded glumly. She had run completely out of breath, and his calmness had increased her rage to the point that she could find nothing else to say.

'I didn't give you the grade, Devon. You earned it.'

She flung the paper on to the desk. 'You've made snide comments all the way through it about my illogical thinking and conclusions not based on fact.'

'It's true that I happen to disagree with many of your conclusions. But you did a beautiful job of stating the problem, and you have a lot of good ideas.' He blew a smoke ring at the ceiling and said, not looking at her, 'In fact, I was so impressed that I almost offered you a job on the strength of it.'

'What kind of job?' she asked uncertainly.

'Doing just that sort of thing. Looking at a problem, considering all the possibilities, writing it all up for me so I can consider it and take a stand. I won't have time to do it all for myself; I'll need some good assistants.'

The lump in Devon's throat was so large it would probably be permanent, she thought. 'Well, aren't you glad that you didn't make that mistake?'

'Very.' His voice was cold.

'I wouldn't have taken it anyway,' she snapped. 'I told you that I hate research. Besides, you're very certain that you're going to need that sort of help. Hadn't you better get elected first? The last I knew it was still necessary to please the voters, not just the party bigwigs.'

'Oh, I'll be elected. You don't need to concern yourself with that.'

'I won't waste a moment's worry on it, believe me. I'm sure you and Bob Dickinson have it all worked out. Now, since I am already late for my class . . .'

His voice pursued her to the door. 'The task force I'll be running for Bob is on drug abuse.'

Devon stopped on the threshold.

'And the drug which is abused most of all, as you pointed out in that paper, is the legal one—alcohol.'

'I'm sure there are all kinds of qualified people to help you.'

'Aren't you sorry that you won't be one of them?' he mused.

Devon turned to face him, and forced a smile. 'Not in the least. I'll be right here, working on my master's degree. I worked hard to get into grad school, and now that I'm in, I wouldn't give it up for any kind of——' she hesitated over her choice of words, then shrugged and said, 'for any kind of job you offered me. Got it Dr Hardesty?'

She didn't stop at the lecture hall; Dr Burton hated to have his classes interrupted, and Devon couldn't have concentrated anyway. Besides, she didn't want to face Matt just yet with that quarrel so fresh; she'd give herself away. It was bad enough that she'd agreed to go to the movie.

No, she told herself then. You will go, and you will have a good time. If you don't, you'll just sit alone in the apartment and brood again. And Jon isn't worth brooding over.

She jumped when a car horn sounded behind her, and looked over her shoulder irritably. She hadn't jaywalked, or anything, so why was the driver honking at her?

The little blue compact was so new that it didn't even have license plates yet. Devon stepped back warily as it pulled up beside her and the door was thrust open.

'I'll give you a ride home,' came a cheery voice, and Devon leaned over to get a better look inside the car.

'Julie! What are you doing with a new car? Where's David's clunker?' She climbed in and took a deep breath of the luscious new-car smell.

Julie laughed and pulled the car back into traffic. 'The clunker has gone to the junkyard where it should have been five years ago.'

'But how did you manage this?'

'It was a wedding present. And you'll never guess from whom.'

'Dad.'

'You're right. We had to take my parents' car on our honeymoon, you know, because David's wasn't safe.

When we came home, the clunker was gone and this was parked in its place.'

'Has David forgiven him?'

'He's talked to C.J. several times. Actually, I think he's glad it happened. It was like a boil, you know.'

'A what?'

Julie looked impatient. 'An infection that was all closed in. It's been a sore spot in his heart for so long. Now that it's been opened up, it can start to heal.'

'I suppose you're right,' Devon said faintly, 'but the comparison makes me a little ill. Promise me that you'll stick to medicine and leave literature alone, all right, Julie?'

Julie laughed. 'All right. But I learned a lesson, along the way. I will have no more secrets from my husband. Ever.'

Devon thought about telling Julie about what Doc had discovered that afternoon, but then she decided that it would be best for David if he didn't know where his tuition money had come from. She felt obligated to make an effort to pay her father back the money he had advanced; David would probably feel the same way, but he would be in no position to do anything about it for years.

'Want to come in for a while?' she asked when Julie parked the little car behind the apartment.

'No. David will be home soon, and it's my turn to start dinner. Why don't you and Jon come over?'

'I think he has plans for tonight. And so do I, come to that. Thanks, anyway, Julie.'

Julie had started to frown. 'Next weekend, then. I'll call you.' She waved and drove off.

'That was close,' Devon told herself. Julie was starting to behave as if they were really living together, instead of just sharing the apartment. 'And right now, we aren't even doing that,' Devon told Cyan as the cat came to strop herself against her ankles. 'And I'm glad.'

Cyan didn't look convinced.

The movie was good, a sentimental comedy with all kinds of misunderstandings and disagreements. Devon cried at the happy ending. Why couldn't life be so simple, she wondered, sniffing a little as they left the theatre.

'Devon, please dry the tears. It wasn't that sad,' Matt pleaded, a little embarrassed to walk through the lobby with her.

'Sorry, Matt.'

'I don't understand, you know,' he said as they started back across campus. The night was clear, and stars sparkled down on to the wide lawns where grass was beginning to show green. 'I thought it was a comedy.'

Devon shrugged. 'It just struck me as being very sad.'

Matt looked as if he didn't believe her, but he didn't pursue the subject. 'Graduation's only four weeks away,' he said.

'I know. I have to pick up my cap and gown next week.'

'Will you be here this summer?'

'No. Oh, no.' Her voice was quick, almost panicky. 'At least, I'll be moving right after graduation.' She certainly couldn't afford to stay in the apartment after Jon moved. She'd leave right now if she hadn't signed that lease. 'I'm looking for something smaller.'

'Not getting along with the roommate?' There was a chuckle in his voice. 'I could have told you to expect that.'

They walked on in silence for another block. She shouldn't have been surprised, either, she thought. But who would have expected Devon Quinn—the girl who had always been the object of the hopeless love affair—to be the one who got hurt? Now that it had happened she was hurt so badly that she wondered if she would ever be the same again.

She looked up at Matt, remembering with surprise how she had been instantly attracted to him. He was good looking, and he was sweet most of the time. But he was only a boy, and after Jon, Devon simply wasn't interested in a boy. She wondered if she could even become interested now in another man—a man who wasn't Jon. A whisper of fear touched her heart.

'You've changed,' Matt said suddenly.

She was startled. 'What do you mean?'

'Last winter, when we first started to see each other, you were pretty straightforward. Now, it's as if there is a whole new part of you that wasn't there before. It's down underneath, where no one can see it. It's kind of like you've grown up this spring.'

'Considering that you've only known me three months . . .' Devon said drily.

Matt laughed. 'Sounds silly, doesn't it? But you didn't deny it.'

'I'm thinking,' she countered. 'Perhaps you're right.' She looked down the street and saw that the apartment was dark. It was beginning to be like the ache of an old wound, this pain that she felt when she came home to empty rooms—rooms that Jon would not be sharing again. The sooner I can move out of that apartment the better, she told herself, and knew underneath that it was only part of an answer.

She considered asking Matt to come in; she'd baked a chocolate cake that afternoon. In the back of her mind rang a tired little refrain. You did it in the hope that Jon would come home and understand that it was an apology. She squelched the thought, and the invitation with it. Matt was no fool; he'd been at Jon's open house. She could hardly expect him to come into the same apartment now and not recognise it.

'Aren't you going to offer me a cup of coffee?' he asked.

'Just coffee?' Devon smiled.

'Well, perhaps a good night kiss, too. But nothing more, I promise.'

'I think not, Matt.'

'Somehow I expected that. I've learned from the experience, you know. You're perfectly safe with me.'

She shook her head sadly. She had no choice, really. All her choices, it seemed, had long ago been made.

He held her hand as they walked around to the back porch. A car pulled into the parking lot next door, and Devon stumbled and stared in horror as the headlights swept across the satin-smooth surface of Jon's green sports car, parked quietly in the dark nook next to the back door.

Oh, my God, she thought. He's here. He must be sitting there in the dark, waiting for me . . .

She could have screamed. How careless could you be, she asked herself, to bring Matt anywhere near. She had assumed because the lights were off that the apartment was empty; it would never have occurred to her to look for his car. If she had decided to invite Matt in . . .

And still, if Jon decided to appear . . . The mood he was in, he might do anything, and he wouldn't like it if he discovered Matt there.

They stood on the back porch in silence for several minutes. Devon's nerves were screaming.

Matt frowned abstractedly and then snapped his fingers. 'Now I remember. This is the building Hardesty lives in. Is that why you two can't get along?'

'It's . . . part of it, Matt.'

'Does he play his stereo too loud or something? Or does he bring home too many women? I knew there was something fishy.'

Devon didn't answer. She was too afraid that if she tried to speak, she would just start crying.

'Is your roommate home tonight?' Matt asked.

Was there a safe answer to that? 'I'm not sure,' Devon stammered finally.

'Devon, are you all right?'

'I'm fine. Truly.'

'I really messed up that night, didn't I?' he said ruefully. 'You're afraid to be alone in a room with me.'

Devon didn't answer. There was no way to explain. Besides, she was straining her ears for any tell-tale sounds from inside, anything that might warn her if Jon was going to suddenly appear.

'I'm sorry, Devon. I really would like to try again.'

When she was still silent, Matt sighed. 'Well, I'll see you around.'

'I'm sorry, Matt. I did enjoy the movie.'

'That's something, at least. If I promise not to get out of hand, can I at least have that good night kiss?'

Devon laughed, a little shakily. 'Of course.'

It was a nice, quiet, gentle kiss, the comfortable kind that she was used to from boyfriends. And, after Jon's kisses, it was totally unsatisfying.

She waved goodbye to him from the back porch and went in, noticing a fresh pot of coffee on the kitchen counter, and the cake, still untouched, beside it. So much for your gesture of reconciliation, Devon told herself.

She locked the door and leaned against it for a moment, trying to gather her strength for the ordeal ahead. Though what made her think it would be an ordeal, she didn't know; perhaps Jon was asleep and had missed the whole thing, or perhaps he simply didn't care what she did or who she was with. That was far more likely, she told herself sadly. Just because she was madly jealous of Margo didn't mean that Jon felt anything at all about Matt.

But he had been upset this afternoon when he saw them together, she argued to herself. Perhaps he had only been thinking her stupid, though, to expose herself to danger.

'Don't kid yourself about being important to him,' she muttered.

'To whom? Matt?'

Devon's eyes popped open; Jon was standing at the

bottom of the stairs, his shoulder propped against the railing, his arms folded across his chest. He looked a little dangerous himself.

'So you're seeing Matt again,' he said softly.

'Is there any reason I shouldn't? You managed to convince me that what he did that night was all my fault.'

Jon started to push himself away from the railing, and Devon felt herself shrink a little. Then he laughed grimly and resettled himself there. Cyan came down the steps, looked them over, and meowed plaintively at Jon's feet. He stooped to pick her up.

Devon wasn't fooled. Just because he was stroking the cat didn't mean that he was any safer to be around.

Anything to get off the subject of Matt, she thought. 'Did you know that Dad was paying for my tuition? And David's?' She moved carefully past him into the living room and leaned against the corner of his desk. With the heavy bulk of it behind her, she felt a little more secure.

Jon followed her. 'I suspected it. He knew an awful lot about your classes and your grades.'

'You didn't tell me.'

Jon shrugged. 'It was only suspicion.'

There was a long silence. Devon finally said, with an effort, 'Look, we have to get through the next four weeks somehow. It's going to be bad enough without us baiting each other. Can we just pretend that things are like they used to be?'

'No.'

She turned away to hide the tears in her eyes. Her hands felt uselessly empty, so she picked up a stack of typed pages, straightening them absent-mindedly.

'Don't touch that,' he said, and his voice was sharp.

Devon spun around, eyes wide in shock, and the manuscript slipped from her hands, spraying over the carpet. 'But it's your book . . .'

'I know quite well what it is. I don't want you to touch it again. Understand?' His voice was so hard that she was stunned.

'I'll pick it up . . .' she murmured.

He had bent to gather some of the pages together. He stood up suddenly, and Devon shrank back against the desk, half-afraid that he would strike her.

He flung the loose pages on the blotter and stood there staring at her. 'Oh, God, Devon, don't look at me like that. Don't be afraid of me.'

'I can't help it when you're like this,' she breathed. 'I don't know you when you're like this.'

'Don't you understand? I want you so much, Devon. So badly that all my reason goes out the window when you refuse me.' He held out a hand, and when she didn't flinch away from him he stroked her cheek gently with one finger, like a child afraid to touch a china doll. 'I won't hurt you, Devon, I promise.'

But you will, she thought. Not physically; no, never that. But the emotional pain . . . the loss when you go away . . . those are things I'll never get over.

He saw the doubt in her eyes, and he sighed heavily. 'I only know that I can't trust myself to stay here,' he said. 'I don't know what I might do, but I'll leave rather than hurt you.'

'You'll go away now?' she whispered.

'I think it's the only safe way for both of us, don't you? I'll let you know where I'm staying. Just don't be afraid of me any more, Devon. I can't stand that.'

When she looked up, he was gone.

Devon stood there for a long time, hearing the noises of packing from upstairs, her mind crying out for time and peace to think. But there was no time, and there would be no peace.

Which was better, she asked herself, four weeks of poisoned happiness followed by bereavement and loneliness, or the same grief with no happy memories at all? If he were dying, would she hesitate? Of course not; she would seize the moment and enjoy what time there was.

You know what you want, Devon, she told herself firmly. Now the question is, are you woman enough to go after it?

CHAPTER TWELVE

SHE picked up the scattered pages of Jon's manuscript, sorting them carefully back into order and stacking them on the corner of his desk again. It took a few minutes, and by the time she had finished, the room upstairs was absolutely silent.

What is it going to be, Devon, she asked herself quietly. But she already knew what she had to do.

She was trembling with fear as she climbed the stairs, fear of what Jon might say to her. And her hand was shaking as she raised it to tap on his door.

'Go away, Devon,' he said.

She pushed the door open and went in.

He was standing at the window, his back to her, his hands buried deep in his pockets. He looked as if he'd like to dismantle something. The room was dark; he hadn't bothered to turn on a light.

Cold shivers were running down her spine as he turned to stare at her. 'Damn it, Devon, I told you to go away.'

Devon closed the door behind her, leaned against it, and looked up at him with quiet defiance in her eyes.

'I'll be ready to leave in a few minutes,' he said wearily. 'Go to your room and shut the door.'

She spoke then, and the quiet tone of her voice belied the word. 'No.'

It seemed to shake him for an instant, then he scowled.

'You told me once,' Devon said, in a tone so quiet it was almost a whisper, 'that if I wanted to learn something, I should look for someone who understood the subject. Well, I'm ready now to learn about making love, and I want you to teach me.'

His scowl deepened. 'Get out of here, Devon.'

'You also said that when I changed my mind I'd have to convince you that I really meant it. What can I do that will be convincing, I wonder?' The question was more to herself than to him.

She walked slowly across to him and let her hands skim up across the hard muscles of his arms. She pressed the whole length of her body against his and pulled his head down, holding his face between her hands. 'Kiss me, Jon—please,' she whispered.

A shiver ran through his body. He raised strong fingers to her cheek, and then pulled away as if the effort was painful. 'Your time is running out.' He stepped back from her and half-turned away.

'We still have four weeks, Jon. I want to spend those precious days with you.'

His face seemed to soften a little, in the shadow. But Devon couldn't tell for sure. And still he didn't move.

She nearly gave up then, but he raised a hand to his collar and tugged on it as if it were too tight.

His voice wasn't as harsh, but it was still firm. 'Get out of this room while you still can.'

'I'm not going to leave, Jon. You'll have to throw me out.' And as if to emphasise her determination, Devon started to undress. She stepped out of her shoes, draped her blazer over the back of a chair, and pulled the hairpins out of the blonde knot at the back of her head. She stood running her fingers through her hair, raising it off her neck, and said, 'Will you unzip my sweater?'

Jon didn't answer. He stayed motionless in the shadow of the window.

Devon sighed and pulled her sweater over her head, laying it atop her jacket. The high-waisted, belted slacks were next; she folded them carefully. Her heart was pounding, but she was trying to be as casual as if she had done this every night for a year.

There was a sudden, violent movement from the window, as if Jon was struggling with himself. Devon smiled, a little secret smile, and her bra and pantyhose joined the pile. She turned towards him then, knowing that the moonlight from the window was gleaming off her naked body.

She moved quietly around the room, turning the blankets back on his bed, fluffing the pillows. She sat down on the edge of the bed and looked up at him. 'Don't you want me, Jon?' she asked, very softly. If you don't, she thought, I'm going to curl up and die right here.

'Oh, God, yes,' he said. It sounded as if the words were being torn from him.

'Then ... what's stopping you?' She held out a hand, and he walked slowly across the room to take it.

'Are you certain, Devon?' he asked, and she nodded.

He hesitated an instant longer, and Devon thought that her heart was pounding so loud that he surely could hear it. Then, his decision made, he began to unbutton his shirt.

Devon propped her elbow on the pillow and watched him. The lean, tall body, without an excess ounce of flesh, the dark, curly mat of hair on his chest, made her fingers itch to touch him.

'Do you like what you see?' he asked drily, and didn't wait for an answer before he bent his head to kiss her.

He was gentle with her, and patient as he showed her the incredible sensations that her body was capable of feeling. She had been afraid that her inexperience would be embarrassing, or that he might even laugh at her. But his patience was inexhaustible.

His touch was like the brush of fire across her delicate skin. Every nerve ending tingled under his kisses. She had been excited by his touch before, but that was nothing compared to this, she thought a little muzzily.

'I may regret this in the morning,' he muttered, and his body tensed against hers. Devon murmured a little protest and pulled him even closer, and Jon sighed and kissed her again.

And then there was no more hesitation from either

of them, no doubt that this was where they belonged, that this was what they had been made for.

The instant of pain she felt was gone so quickly that Devon thought she might have imagined it. She had no time to wonder, then, as they found their way together to the ecstasy that seemed to leave them weightless and timeless.

Much later, as she lay dreamily in his arms, she said, 'I thought they were exaggerating.'

Jon let his fingers trail down the curve of her throat and toy with the fullness of her breast as he asked, 'Who? And what?'

'The girls who told me how glorious sex was. I thought they were just making it up so the rest of us would be jealous.'

He laughed at that. 'Glorious, hmm?'

'If I'd known,' she said lazily, 'I wouldn't have waited so long.'

'Does that mean you'd have slept with Matt that night? Because if it does I ought to spank you,' Jon threatened.

'It isn't Matt I want,' she said indistinctly and tumbled off into exhausted sleep, cradled in his arms, secure for the moment. Her last thought was of the precious few weeks to come, and now they could make the most of their time together.

When she woke and stretched and found herself in his bed, all the pleasure of the night before came flooding back to her, so that she was smiling softly when she turned to Jon.

He was awake, but there were two sharp lines between his eyes. He looked worried.

Devon tried to brush his frown away. 'Are you regretting it this morning?' she asked gently.

He didn't answer, but his scowl deepened.

'Please don't,' she whispered. 'It was beautiful, Jon. And don't be afraid that I'm going to expect more from you than you can give. In four weeks you're going away, and I'm staying here. I know that. It's all right for us to enjoy this month, darling. You called it an interlude . . .'

He pushed her away and slipped out of bed. She watched, puzzled, as he pulled on his jogging clothes.

'Jon?' she questioned, becoming frightened at his silence.

He laced his shoes with what seemed unnecessary violence. 'I need some time to think, Devon,' he said, and left the room without a backward glance. Two minutes later she heard the back door slam.

Devon closed her eyes against the black pain in her soul. She had begged him to make love to her, and he had not been able to refuse her. He was not superhuman, after all, and she had thrown herself at him. Last night had been magic, but this morning was Margo.

Devon had forgotten about Margo, but Jon could not. It was easy for Devon to plan that little interlude, just the two of them in a springtime Eden. But Margo wasn't going to disappear. And if she found out, if she told her father, the consequences to Jon would be lifelong.

Devon pushed the blankets back, leaving them in a careless heap, and snatched up her clothes from the chair where she had left them so carefully folded the night before. She stood under the shower for a long time, her tears mingling with the hot spray, wanting to scrub herself till every trace of Jon was washed away, and knowing with the deepest fibre of her being that it was impossible, that the memories of last night would always be with her.

And that was what you wanted, she told herself drearily as she dressed. You wanted memories; you have them. And you thought it would be easier to do without him if only he had made love to you, she told herself angrily. What a fool you are, Devon Quinn.

She went downstairs, glancing at her watch. Jon

seldom returned from his morning jog in less than an hour; she still had a few minutes to escape.

Escape? Yes, she told herself, that was the right word. The night that had been everything to her was a nightmare to Jon, and that she could not bear. She shrugged, and feeling a need to be close to something, she picked up the cat. Cyan meowed loudly in protest and jumped out of Devon's arms to the windowsill where she straightened her fur in offended dignity.

Even the cat had rejected her, Devon thought moodily.

She began to pull dying leaves off the plants hanging in the bay window. She was in a mood to destroy something, but she stopped herself. It wasn't the fault of the plants, that was sure.

Anger stirred deep inside her, anger at herself. Why should she have expected that making love to her would be anything special to Jon? She had been an awestruck virgin; he was—Devon told herself that she would prefer not to think about all the beautiful women Jon had known, and slept with.

The whole world looked unfamiliar this morning, she thought, looking out the living room window at the dirty landscape. The snow had melted in all but the shadowed areas, leaving dust, sand and salt from the long winter. Though it was April, the rains hadn't come yet to wash away the grime and clear the way for new, clean growth.

A good day to be gloomy, Devon thought, and jumped as the back door opened. Too late now to run, she thought. She couldn't escape without him hearing her. Unless he went upstairs to shower—then she could slip out.

He didn't. She heard water running in the kitchen, and then there was silence. She would have to brave his presence; she certainly couldn't hover in the living room indefinitely. But she continued to stand there as if suspended, almost without breathing.

The coffee had finished perking by the time Devon

forced herself to the kitchen doorway. Jon looked up as he poured a cup and stared at her as if he'd never seen her before.

Devon swallowed hard and reached for her coffee mug. By the time she had filled it, Jon had turned away and sat down at the kitchen table. She kept her back to him as she spooned sugar into the strong dark brew.

Then she said, over her shoulder, 'I'm sorry about last night. I just want you to know that I don't blame you for anything. I threw myself at you, and I got what I deserved.'

There was a long silence, and Devon stirred her coffee till she was afraid she'd wear a hole in the bottom of the cup. Finally Jon said, his voice carefully neutral, 'I'm not sure I understand.'

Devon's hand clenched on the spoon. 'Jon, it was fairly obvious this morning. Look, I may be innocent, but I'm not dumb. It couldn't have been too much fun for you last night, and I'm sorry, all right?' She was fighting tears.

His chair scraped on the floor. Devon stood very still.

He pried the spoon out of her hand and tossed it with a flick of his wrist into the sink. His hand closed around her arm and spun her towards him. The set expression on his face frightened her.

'Jon?' she whispered.

'You gave me a very precious gift last night, Devon. You deserve to know just how precious it is to me.'

The touch of his hands was enough to set her on fire. Devon was finding it difficult to breathe; just being near him was making her tremble. Then, very gently, he tipped her face up to his and kissed her, tenderly, almost reverently.

It wasn't enough. Deep in her throat Devon made a little primitive sound and pulled him even closer, as if by sheer physical strength she could absorb him and keep him forever with her.

Jon kissed her hard and set her aside. He was

breathing with difficulty. 'You are so very innocent,' he said, and to Devon's ears it sounded like an accusation. 'You don't even know that it isn't like this for everyone.'

She leaned against the counter. 'It isn't?'

He shook his head. 'No, it isn't. Last night wasn't fun for me, Devon. It was more like a revelation— something I'd never expected to find.'

'Then . . .'

'I don't regret that you tempted me. But now it becomes difficult, Devon. I can't give up my job, you see. I promised Bob that I'd come back to Washington; I can't back out now.'

Devon wasn't interested. He had told her what she needed to hear—that she was desirable and attractive and that he wanted her. She'd worry about the rest later, she decided. 'It doesn't matter, Jon. It really doesn't. We have a whole month . . .'

'You don't understand, Devon. You can't just compress all of life and loving into thirty days and then pull the plug at the end of it.'

He does want me, she thought, a little dazed. He does.

'It would be better to stop now than to try to call a halt after four weeks of nights like last night. Affairs like this one don't burn out that fast, and it won't work, with me in Washington and you here. Trust me, Devon; I know.'

She had buried her head against his shoulder, trying to shut out the words he was saying. She knew he was right, but a tiny voice in the back of her mind kept insisting that she had to fight for what she wanted. Margo would have him for life; all Devon was asking was four short weeks, to carry her through a lifetime.

How frightened he must be, she thought, that she wouldn't give him up at the end of the month. She tried to reassure him. 'I won't try to hold you,' she said breathlessly. 'I'll let you go—you said you wanted to have an affair with me . . .'

'I still do. But things have changed, Devon.'

Of course. He couldn't indulge in an affair right now; to do so would risk enraging Margo, breaking off his engagement, ruining the promise of his new job. Unhappiness swept over her. Was this the price she had to pay for one night's glory?

'Come with me,' he said. 'There are graduate schools in Washington . . .'

'You must be crazy,' she said. Share him with Margo? Know that when he came to visit her in some little apartment that Margo was waiting for him across town? Read in the papers each day about Margo's parties, Margo's successes—Margo as Mrs Jonathan Hardesty?

No. She could bear being parted from him. But she couldn't bear that.

She shook her head. 'I'm going to stay here and get my degree, Jon. And then I'm going somewhere to teach. Maybe I'll go to California; Dad will help me find a job, and I've always wanted to see it.'

He was silent, and she stumbled on, 'I'm only asking for these few weeks to remember. I can be discreet, Jon . . .'

His hands clenched her shoulders. 'Stop and think, Devon! Can you really be content for us to sleep together for four weeks and then never see each other again?'

Never? The prospect was so horrifying that it shook Devon to the bottom of her soul. 'Maybe we could see each other sometimes . . .' she said uncertainly. 'You'll be travelling . . .'

'Damn it, no. Don't you hear what I'm saying?'

Fury blazed to life deep inside her. 'Why can't you trust me?' she cried. 'It would be too much of a risk to your career, is that what's bothering you? It's dragged down a lot of politicians, that's sure. And of course it isn't going to be allowed to happen to you, is it, Jon? When it comes down to what's really important to you, it's always the politics that wins, isn't it?'

Her words fell into a silence that was so deep it frightened her. They seemed to echo in the stillness of the kitchen.

It was a full five minutes later when Jon said, 'What exactly is it that you want, Devon?'

'I want to have a few weeks of happiness with you. That's all. I know you have to go to Washington, and that I have to stay here. I know that it will be over in four short weeks. I don't want to hurt your career. I will not stand in the way of you doing whatever you need to do.'

Even if it is to marry Margo? her other self questioned. Yes, she answered firmly. Even that. Because if I can have him for these few weeks, then a part of him will always belong to me.

'I care about you,' she finished quietly, 'and I want to have some memories of you.'

'Just how damn much do you care, if you won't come with me?' he asked bitterly. 'I'm not asking you to give up your education, just to finish school somewhere else.'

Devon stared at him for a moment that seemed to stretch out forever. How could he ask her that question, she wondered. Her whole body ached; she felt as if she was tearing herself apart. She looked up at the kitchen clock and said quietly, 'I have a class in fifteen minutes.'

He looked startled. 'So do I. Give me five minutes in the shower and I'll drop you off.' He ran a hand over his rumpled dark hair. 'I'll be lucky if I can remember the topic—much less whatever it is I planned to say about it. But I'd better show up.'

'No, thanks. I'll feel better for the walk.' She stood in the doorway, zipping her coat, feeling as if there was so much yet to say—and not knowing what it was she wanted to tell him. Finally she said, 'Goodbye, Jon.'

'Does that mean you aren't coming back?'

'I don't know right now. We don't seem to have much hope of working it out, do we?'

He was silent, and she shut the door quietly behind her and walked through the frosty cold towards the campus.

She didn't even notice the humid air or the heavy clouds hanging over her, promising to bring more snow, despite what the calendar said. She felt only the stabbing pain in her heart.

She knew she was right to refuse to go with him. Jon's morals would be under scrutiny continually; a brief affair was forgivable, but if he was keeping a mistress across town from his wife it would be begging for a scandal.

And yet . . .

She might as well not have wasted time in the classroom that day. She walked from room to room in a daze and remembered nothing from the lectures. She did notice, about noon, that it had started to snow. An April blizzard, she thought; that was all she needed to make it a perfectly dreadful day. But she was too absorbed in her own difficult decision to really care.

Doc Driscoll had another student in his office when Devon stopped by. She knew it was rude to interrupt, but she did it anyway. 'Doc,' she asked, leaning around the doorframe, 'if I decide to move, can I transfer into another graduate school?'

'Depends on where you go. Maybe, but it's like starting from the beginning, and it's awfully late.' He studied her with sharp eyes. 'Where are you moving to? California, with your father?'

'I've thought about it.' She wasn't about to confide in Doc; he'd think she had really lost her mind. Devon wasn't so certain that she hadn't.

'Well, be smart enough to wait till next year, all right? Hang around and I'll talk to you in a minute.'

She didn't wait. She went out into the heavy, wet snow and walked for a long time, in a daze, looking up in surprise much later to find herself at the door of

Portable Pies. And only then did she realise how cold she was—frozen, it seemed, clear to the heart.

She sat down at a table near the windows, and stared thoughtfully out across the broad street to the lighted window that had started it all—the window of their living room, where the sign had declared that the apartment was for rent.

If I could go back to that day, Devon thought, I'd ignore that sign and run as fast as I could . . .

But she wouldn't have run away, she knew. She wouldn't change anything, because loving Jon was worth all the pain. The waitress brought her a mug of hot apple cider, and Devon sat stirring it with a cinnamon stick, staring out into the snowstorm and thinking about the echoes of fate. Two people had shared a table at Portable Pies on that snowy afternoon three months ago, and their lives were changed forever.

Well, at least mine has been, she amended. As Margo had once told her, Jon didn't waste time on memories, and that was all Devon could ever be for him.

Or did she still have choices after all? What would happen if she did go with him? If that was the only way she could have him, could she take it on faith that the love she felt for him would carry her over the rough times? Could they be discreet enough so that his career would not be in danger?

Could she trust him? She was surprised to find that there was nothing but confidence in her heart. Margo might have his name, but she would never know the essence of the man—the hidden Jon Hardesty that he had never really shared with anyone before. That part of him would always be Devon's.

A tall, dark-haired man came in, shaking the snow off the shoulders of his trenchcoat. Devon shrank back in her chair, but it was impossible to disappear. Jon waited at the counter for his coffee, and carried it over to her table.

'May I sit down?' he asked quietly.

Devon nodded. 'You don't have a taco today,' she said, and then felt a little foolish for bringing up the past.

He sipped his coffee and said suddenly, 'What if I stay here for one more year?'

'You can't.'

'I've been offered a contract with the university. Burton's retiring—I can start as an assistant professor.'

Devon's heart leaped with joy. To have him here . . .

She stirred her cider and looked up with misty eyes. 'What would you tell Bob Dickinson, Jon? You can't turn him down.'

'Yes, I can. There will be other jobs in Washington.'

She shook her head, and wondered if the pain and tightness in her chest was what it felt like when a heart was breaking. 'That kind of offer only comes once. If you don't take it now, he'll find someone else to nurture and promote, and when election time comes . . .' Her voice broke.

Jon shrugged. 'Then that's the way it will have to be.'

She looked up at him with disbelief. 'You would do that, Jon? You'd give up politics?'

'I don't think I could, Devon. Not entirely—it's in my blood. But I can postpone it for a year, wait till your degree is finished, then go back. It might make it harder, but Bob will understand.'

Devon was glad that he was so certain he could explain it to Bob Dickinson. She hoped that she didn't have to overhear that conversation. Or the one with Margo; she wondered what he planned to tell his fiancée. 'I'm that important to you?' she whispered.

He sighed. 'It doesn't seem very exciting any more, if you aren't there to share it with. Seems a little foolish, doesn't it? But if that damned degree is so important to you . . .'

Devon blotted tears away with her napkin and tried to find her voice. He would give up what had been the most important thing in his life in order to stay with her?

'I'll go with you,' she said, and the quiet words seemed to ring out: 'You don't have to wait a year; I'll go with you now.'

He looked stunned. 'You will?'

She nodded, and waited for fear and shock to strike her, but they didn't. All she felt was a deep sense of relief. Her decision was made; right or wrong, she was content with it.

'There's a price, Devon,' he warned. 'If we stay together at all, it has to be on my terms.'

Don't tell me about Margo, she thought. I don't want my happiness clouded with her right now, or with the rules of how to play the game. Just let me have a few minutes to dream about how beautiful it could be . . .

'It takes three days to get married in this state,' Jon said briskly. 'And I don't want to waste any time. If your father can't come this weekend, I don't think we should wait.'

'Married?' Devon asked faintly.

He reached for her hands across the table. 'Look, I know neither of us has much respect for it. Your parents had a rotten marriage and so have mine. But if I am going to be in the public eye, there will be horrid things said about me anyway. But you will be the one untouchable thing in my life—the one thing they can't say anything bad about.'

'Marriage?' she repeated.

Jon hurried on, 'Maybe if we just think of it as being a legal move that doesn't have to get in the way of our friendship . . .'

Devon interrupted. 'What about Margo?'

He frowned. 'What about her?'

'You're engaged to her.'

'Who told you that?'

'She did. She said that she was going to marry you.' Devon's head was spinning.

'Did she actually say I'd proposed to her?'

Devon tried to remember. 'I don't know. I thought she did.'

'That's been a fond dream of hers for five years. I disillusion her every now and then, but it keeps coming back.' He raised the palm of her hand to his lips. 'Just what in the hell did you think I meant, anyway?'

His breath tickled her palm. 'That you wanted to have an affair with me. That's what you kept saying.'

'So I did.' The light in his eyes brought hot colour to her cheeks. 'It just took me a while to realise that an affair wasn't enough. What about it, wench? Do you want to be an honest woman?'

'What about your job with Bob Dickinson? If you don't marry Margo . . .'

'Bob will tell me that I have a great deal of sense. She may be his daughter, but he has no blind spots about her.'

'And your parents. They expect a grand marriage for you . . .'

'Even my father doesn't really care who I marry, as long as I do it soon. But he thinks you're charming. Not too many women are willing to argue with him.' He pulled her to her feet and held her coat. 'Shall we go call C.J. and invite him to another wedding?'

Devon's mind was still spinning. 'But . . . why didn't you tell me you wanted to marry me?'

'Because you kept talking about the next four weeks as if you couldn't bear to put up with me any longer than that. And all spring you've been telling me that only a crazy woman would get married. You still haven't answered me, dammit.'

'Yes, Jon.' There were stars in her eyes.

He seized her hand. 'Let's get out of here before I scandalise the whole campus.'

On the sidewalk Devon stopped dead and stared up at him.

'What is it now?' he demanded.

Her eyes were enormous. 'I forgot to pay for my apple cider,' she confessed.

His laugh rang out through the frosty air. 'I see I have no choice about running for president,' he mused. 'You need a Secret Service agent assigned to take care of the details you can't seem to remember. Devon, my darling . . .'

The snow formed a curtain around them, shutting them off from the world.

WORLDWIDE LIBRARY IS YOUR TICKET TO ROMANCE, ADVENTURE AND EXCITEMENT

Experience it all in these big, bold Bestsellers— Yours exclusively from WORLDWIDE LIBRARY WHILE QUANTITIES LAST

To receive these Bestsellers, complete the order form, detach and send together with your check or money order (include 75¢ postage and handling), payable to WORLDWIDE LIBRARY, to:

In the U.S.
WORLDWIDE LIBRARY
Box 52040
Phoenix, AZ
85072-2040

In Canada
WORLDWIDE LIBRARY
P.O. Box 2800, 5170 Yonge Street
Postal Station A, Willowdale, Ontario
M2N 6J3

Quant.	Title	Price
_____	**WILD CONCERTO**, Anne Mather	$2.95
_____	**A VIOLATION**, Charlotte Lamb	$3.50
_____	**SECRETS**, Sheila Holland	$3.50
_____	**SWEET MEMORIES**, LaVyrle Spencer	$3.50
_____	**FLORA**, Anne Weale	$3.50
_____	**SUMMER'S AWAKENING**, Anne Weale	$3.50
_____	**FINGER PRINTS**, Barbara Delinsky	$3.50
_____	**DREAMWEAVER**, Felicia Gallant/Rebecca Flanders	$3.50
_____	**EYE OF THE STORM**, Maura Seger	$3.50
_____	**HIDDEN IN THE FLAME**, Anne Mather	$3.50
	ECHO OF THUNDER, Maura Seger	$3.95
_____	**DREAM OF DARKNESS**, Jocelyn Haley	$3.95
	YOUR ORDER TOTAL	$_____
	New York and Arizona residents add appropriate sales tax	$_____
	Postage and Handling	$ .75
	I enclose	$_____

NAME _____

ADDRESS _____ APT.# _____

CITY _____

STATE/PROV. _____ ZIP/POSTAL CODE _____

WW3

Coming Next Month in Harlequin Romances!

2749 A MATTER OF MARNIE Rosemary Badger
Convincing an Australian construction tycoon that his
grandmother has been neglected is a formidable task. Living with
him in order to care for the woman is an even greater challenge.

2750 THE PERFECT CHOICE Melissa Forsythe
A voice student in Vienna seldom turns men's heads. So when a
handsome stranger woos her, she's in too deep by the time she
discovers his motive for choosing her over her beautiful friend.

2751 SAFE HARBOUR Rosalie Henaghan
This trustworthy secretary weathers her boss's changeable moods
until his woman friend predicts an end to Anna's working days—
and sets out to make her prophecy come true.

2752 NEVER THE TIME AND THE PLACE Betty Neels
The consulting surgeon at a London hospital disturbs his ward sister's
natural serenity. She's having enough trouble coping with a broken
engagement without having to put up with his arrogance.

2753 A WILL TO LOVE Edwina Shore
That the family's Queensland homestead should be sold is
unthinkable. But the only way to save it—according to her
grandfather's will—is to marry the same man who rejected her
four years ago.

2754 HE WAS THE STRANGER Sheila Strutt
The manager of Milk River Ranch knew that a male relative would
inherit her uncle's spread. But why did the beneficiary have to be a
writer who would either sell out or take over completely?

What readers say about Harlequin romance fiction...

"I absolutely adore Harlequin romances!
They are fun and relaxing to read, and
each book provides a wonderful escape."
    —N.E.,* Pacific Palisades, California

"Harlequin is the best in romantic reading."
    —K.G.,* Philadelphia, Pennsylvania

"Harlequins have been my passport to the
world. I have been many places without
ever leaving my doorstep."
    —P.Z.,* Belvedere, Illinois

"My praise for the warmth and adventure
your books bring into my life."
    —D.F.,* Hicksville, New York

"A pleasant way to relax after a busy day."
    —P.W.,* Rector, Arkansas

*Names available on request.

What the press says about Harlequin romance fiction...

"When it comes to romantic novels...
Harlequin is the indisputable king."
— *New York Times*

"...always with an upbeat, happy ending."
— *San Francisco Chronicle*

"Women have come to trust these
stories about contemporary people,
set in exciting foreign places."
— *Best Sellers*, New York

"The most popular reading matter of
American women today."
— *Detroit News*

"...a work of art."
— *Globe & Mail*, Toronto

Can you keep a secret?

You can keep this one plus 4 free novels

Experience the warmth of ...

Harlequin Romance

**The original romance novels.
Best-sellers for more than 30 years.**

Delightful and intriguing love stories
by the world's foremost writers
of romance fiction.

Be whisked away to dazzling
international capitals ...
or quaint European villages.
Experience the joys of falling in love ...
for the first time, the best time!

Harlequin Romance

**A uniquely absorbing journey
into a world of superb romance reading.**

Wherever paperback books are sold, or through
Harlequin Reader Service

In the U.S.
2504 West Southern Avenue
Tempe, AZ 85282

In Canada
P.O. Box 2800, Postal Station A
5170 Yonge Street
Willowdale, Ontario M2N 6J3

**No one touches the heart of a woman
quite like Harlequin!**

R-111

*You're invited to accept
4 books and a
surprise gift Free!*

Acceptance Card

Mail to: **Harlequin Reader Service**®

In the U.S.
901 Fuhrmann Blvd.
P.O. Box 1394
Buffalo, N.Y. 14240-1394

In Canada
P.O. Box 2800, Postal Station A
5170 Yonge Street
Willowdale, Ontario M2N 6J3

YES! Please send me 4 free Harlequin Presents® novels and my free surprise gift. Then send me 8 brand new novels every month as they come off the presses. Bill me at the low price of $1.75 each ($1.95 in Canada)—an 11% saving off the retail price. There are no shipping, handling or other hidden costs. There is no minimum number of books I must purchase. I can always return a shipment and cancel at any time. Even if I never buy another book from Harlequin, the 4 free novels and the surprise gift are mine to keep forever.

108 BPP-BPGE

_____

Name   (PLEASE PRINT)

_____

Address   Apt. No.

_____

City   State/Prov.   Zip/Postal Code

This offer is limited to one order per household and not valid to present subscribers. Price is subject to change.   ACP-SUB-1R